# DETACHED

# DETACHED

## CHRISTINA KILBOURNE

**DUNDURN**
TORONTO

Editor: Cheryl Hawley
Design: Courtney Horner
Cover design: Sarah Beaudin
Cover image: vectorarts/iStock
Printer: Webcom

**Library and Archives Canada Cataloguing in Publication**

Kilbourne, Christina, 1967-, author
        Detached / Christina Kilbourne.

Issued in print and electronic formats.
ISBN 978-1-4597-3431-9 (paperback).--ISBN 978-1-4597-3432-6 (pdf).--
ISBN 978-1-4597-3433-3 (epub)

        I. Title.

PS8571.I476D48 2016          jC813'.6          C2015-907490-8
                                               C2015-907491-6


1   2   3   4   5       20   19   18   17   16

We acknowledge the support of the **Canada Council for the Arts** and the **Ontario Arts Council** for our publishing program. We also acknowledge the financial support of the **Government of Canada** through the **Canada Book Fund** and **Livres Canada Books**, and the **Government of Ontario** through the **Ontario Book Publishing Tax Credit** and the **Ontario Media Development Corporation.**

Care has been taken to trace the ownership of copyright material used in this book. The author and the publisher welcome any information enabling them to rectify any references or credits in subsequent editions.

— *J. Kirk Howard, President*

The publisher is not responsible for websites or their content unless they are owned by the publisher.

Printed and bound in Canada.

VISIT US AT
Dundurn.com | @dundurnpress | Facebook.com/dundurnpress | Pinterest.com/dundurnpress

Dundurn
3 Church Street, Suite 500
Toronto, Ontario, Canada
M5E 1M2

*For Melanie, with love and admiration*

# ANNA

Even before I realized what was happening, the bridge took over my brain. When I was falling asleep at night I'd see it in my mind until I wanted to stuff my eye sockets full of cotton balls to block out the image. I'd catch glimpses of it during the day too, but it wasn't as obvious, just something hovering at the edge of my peripheral vision. Whenever I had a chance, I started going to the bridge. I'd walk across the city and stare at it from different angles: from up high on the riverbank, from below, from the sidewalk leading across it. But if I was alone, I never got too close.

Then I started sketching it: in pencil, in charcoal, in oil pastel. I even doodled it during math class. Finally, I painted it in acrylics for my year-end portfolio. I'm not even sure I meant to paint it, but there it was at the end of June on a super-sized canvas. It made my stomach heave whenever I saw it across the room and I wished I'd never painted it. My best friend, Aliya, said it was probably the best painting ever to come out of Bachman School for the Arts and that she should know since she was in the visual arts stream too. My teacher said it was stunning, yet disturbing. She said it was mature and showed an impressive use of diffused light. Even though it's supposed to be an honour to be chosen for the year-end student exhibit, I was horrified when she said she wanted it for the centre wall. I asked her to reconsider, suggested one of my classmate's paintings instead. I said I was afraid it wasn't good enough and that people wouldn't appreciate it, but she just waved me away and said something about my false modesty.

Kyle, one of the performance arts guys, was as obsessed with my painting as I was with the bridge itself. He came down to the art room every day to see the painting take shape. He would stand back and stare at it with an intensity that made me nervous. I was afraid he knew what was going on inside me.

"It's almost like it's alive," he said at the exhibit when all the parents and students were sipping apple cider and mingling among our masterpieces.

"It's just a bridge," I said, and thought how ironic that I could paint something so alive when inside I felt the opposite.

"It's not just a bridge anymore. Now it's something more: a story waiting to be told."

"Deep," I said, then immediately regretted it. I hadn't meant to sound sarcastic when he was trying to be nice.

"Whatever it is, I wish I could paint like that. I can hardly draw stick figures," he said.

"I wish I could dance," I countered, deadpan. "I have three left feet." I winced. I felt like I was in kindergarten again and trying too hard to fit in. I could never find the right balance when I talked to him. I was either too reserved or too outgoing. I felt like a basketball bouncing out of control.

Kyle smiled. I wanted to smile back, but it took too long to pull up the corners of my mouth, and by the time I did he'd melted into the crowd. I spent the rest of the night wishing I wasn't such a misfit and that it was time to go home. If it wasn't for the fact I had a painting there, nobody but Kyle and Aliya would have said a word to me.

When the exhibit ended, I took the painting home and hid it in the darkest corner of the basement. I told my parents I gave it to my teacher because she liked it so much. I could tell Mom was disappointed. But I thought that if the painting was out of sight, maybe I could forget about the bridge altogether. I was wrong though. I couldn't get it out of my mind. I started to think that if I walked out on it, and felt it under my feet, I might get over my obsession. You know when you are crushing on someone you don't know very well, then you go out together once and realize it's all wrong? I thought maybe if I spent some time there, if I actually touched it and walked across it, I'd get over it. Or maybe I had other plans, I can't say for sure. I just knew I had to go.

It was summer by the time I made up my mind to walk across the bridge. I had the day off work, Dad was leaving early for a business trip, and Mom had a morning shift at the medical lab where she tests blood and urine and also does the bookkeeping. That gave me a free morning, when nobody would be expecting to see me. So I set my alarm ridiculously early and got up just as the sky was turning from black to grey.

Dad was eating breakfast when I came downstairs. Sherlock was lying at his feet and thumped his tail when he saw me. I was surprised, and annoyed, to see Dad was still home. I'd wanted to be alone.

"I thought you were leaving last night on the red-eye?" I said.

"They called and said they were moving my meeting to after lunch, so your mother wanted me to stay the night."

I nodded and stood awkwardly at the edge of the room.

"What are you doing up so early? I thought you had the day off," he said finally.

"I do. I'm going for a walk before it gets too hot."

Dad looked back at his breakfast. I knew I had to do something that looked halfway normal so I went to the fridge and took out the jug of orange juice. I poured myself a glass, even though I didn't want a drink.

"I made poached eggs. You want me to make you some? The water's still hot."

"I'm not hungry. I'll just have some juice."

"Suit yourself," he said and finished sopping up egg yolk with his last triangle of toast.

Just the sight of eggs first thing in the morning made me want to vomit and the juice felt like battery acid in my stomach.

"What can I bring you back from LA?" he asked playfully.

"I dunno." I said, wishing he'd stop trying to force a conversation so early in the morning and when I had so much dragging me down.

"A snow globe?" he teased.

I scowled but didn't comment. When I was a kid I collected snow globes from all of his business trips. I know it's cliché, but I loved them. I thought they were perfect little worlds and I ached to get inside one so I could finally belong. I had twenty-two snow globes until last year. Then I donated them all to a charity. He came into my room after a trip to San Francisco with a snow globe of the Golden Gate Bridge in his hand. He looked at the empty shelf, then at me, confused.

"I outgrew them," I muttered that day, without looking up from my laptop.

He left the room without saying a word. I saw the snow globe in the garbage later but we never spoke about it. Maybe I should have picked it up and kept it. It might have kept my bridge obsession under control.

"I know. No more snow globes. I'm just kidding. I'll find you something else," he said. He leaned over and squeezed my shoulder.

"I don't want anything," I said suddenly and with too much anger in my voice. I couldn't see the point of collecting more stuff I didn't need and would never use.

Dad stopped and looked at me for a moment. Then he put his dishes in the sink.

"Are you okay?" he asked.

"I'm fine. I just don't need any more crap cluttering up my life."

He reached over as if to feel my forehead, but I batted his hand away. I didn't know if he was being sympathetic or making a joke, but I wasn't in the mood for either. And I didn't wait to find out. I gulped back my juice and bolted for the front door. I knew if I stayed we'd end up in an argument and I wanted to be left alone. I heaved a sigh of relief when he didn't call out after me or follow me through the living room. For the moment I was free to escape.

Stepping outside was like walking into the Amazon pavilion at the zoo. The temperature hadn't cooled at all overnight and it was still humid. It was so hot and sticky, my skin felt coated in glue. I walked down the driveway wearing just a pair of shorts and a tank top, my sandals slapping the pavement.

It's not officially called suicide bridge, but that's what the locals call it because at least three people a year throw themselves into the river below. The last person was some guy who was losing custody of his kids. He left a note blaming his ex-wife for everything that went wrong in his life and took the long dive down. They found his body the next day. It turns out he was a diagnosed schizophrenic.

The bridge is about an hour's walk from our house, but since my feet felt like they were made of concrete, I knew it would take me longer. After ten minutes of struggling along the sidewalk, my forehead was slick with sweat. I wiped it off with my forearm and slowed down even more. I started to doubt myself. I even considered turning around and going back to bed. But then I heard it calling attention to itself, like a distant drumbeat.

It was a hazy day and the city was reluctant to wake up. There wasn't even much traffic. Just one car waited at the lights at the end of our street and only two taxis passed me as I left our neighbourhood. I'd planned it that way. Because the bridge links downtown with the university campus, I figured if I got there early I'd have a better chance of being alone than if I went in the middle of the night.

I could see the top of the bridge as I crested the hill on Melborn Avenue. I could see the sturdy metal arches and thick cement railings. The best part about suicide bridge is the barrier separating the foot traffic from the car traffic so drivers can't see who they are driving past. I'd checked this out specifically before when we'd driven over to visit my brother, Joe.

As I got closer, I saw the river was covered in fog, which made the bridge look like it was floating. I shivered, even though there wasn't a breeze. Before I stepped onto the bridge, I stopped and took a deep breath. Nobody had ever survived a jump. The bridge was high enough that the impact killed people, not drowning.

When you drive over the bridge in a car, it only takes three minutes without traffic, but walking made me realize just how long the distance was. I didn't dare look down, but stared straight ahead at the sidewalk, the railings confining my view. The slapping of my sandals echoed in the silence and I felt a blister forming on the back of my left heel.

At the middle of the bridge there's a small alcove jutting out over the river. The city planners put it there in the early 1900s so people had a good view of downtown. The bridge was a tourist attraction back then, with benches, flower-pots, and garbage cans. But that was thirteen years before someone thought to hurl themselves off it, before the big stock market crash in 1929. I know all this because my art teacher's husband told me at the year-end art exhibit. I stood there for twenty minutes pretending I cared. Now there are no benches on the bridge. There are no flowers and there is no place to put your trash either. The city planners want people to walk straight across these days, without stopping to gawk. In fact, they've made plans to build a cage over the sidewalk to keep people from jumping, but that's still in the early stages.

When I got to the alcove, I stepped close to the railing and peered down. The distance thundered in my head. The fog was beginning to clear and I saw patches of the water below. From where I stood the water appeared to be standing still, but I knew from being at the base of the bridge that it rushes past. It goes fast enough to deliver a body to the outskirts of the city in a few hours.

I leaned against the railing and felt the cool cement through my tank top. I felt the pebbly roughness against the underside of my arms. I imagined what the kids at school would say if I jumped. I wondered how Aliya would react. I knew she'd never understand. She was too much of a fighter to ever consider giving up on anything. Of course, I knew she'd miss me to start, but she had Mariam and Gisele for support. And she had Kyle.

The water churned below and my stomach started to churn with it. My grandparents died in the same river, the same water. I wondered what they thought in the final moments of their lives, when they saw the road disappear and the river rise up before their eyes. I wondered if they held hands and held their breath or scrambled at the windows to get out. I thought quickly about my parents and Joe, about how much they'd suffered after my grandparents died. I wasn't sure I could make them suffer more, but then again, I wasn't sure how much more suffering I could take either.

I let my chin rest on the railing and stared down, mesmerized by the vertical drop, pulled by the power of gravity. How easy it would be, a few seconds of terror and then sweet, beautiful release. I wouldn't even have to jump, I realized, just roll myself over the edge. I wondered how long it would take to lose consciousness — probably only a few short seconds. I counted to ten in my head. It would be over already if I just had the courage, but something kept me rooted in place.

"You okay, miss?"

I looked up, startled to see a tall, lean man with long leg muscles. He was standing back a few feet from the railing, shrouded in the hazy morning. He was dressed in loose shorts and a mesh T-shirt and, with the sun rising behind him, he looked angelic. I'd forgotten about the early-morning fitness enthusiasts.

"Uh, yeah," I said. "I was just feeling a little nauseous."

"Maybe it's the vertigo. Happens to me too. That's why I stand back from the edge and don't look over."

I nodded slowly, tried not to let on how strong the pull was to barrel roll my body over that railing.

"Uh, listen, you look kind of pale. Are you sure you're okay?"

I meant to nod again, but I couldn't tell if my head was moving or not. He stepped toward me and touched my elbow.

"Why don't you walk with me for a minute? It might help clear your head."

It took a great deal of effort to move my right foot forward. I stepped once, twice, then my body was able to remember the pattern and keep the momentum. The jogger walked beside me, watching my face.

"I just live on the other side if you want to come and rest. Maybe you can call home for a ride," he suggested kindly and pointed off in the distance.

I looked up at him, at the concern in his eyes, at the wrinkles bunched up between his eyebrows. I shook my head.

"I'm going to meet my brother for breakfast. He's at the university."

I hoped my lie seemed credible. I mean, this man was a complete stranger and there was no way I wanted to go anywhere with him. Sure, maybe sometimes I wanted to stop existing, but I didn't want some creep to murder me.

"Okay, but just stay away from the railing. It's a long way down," he said and started jogging lightly on the spot.

Before he left I managed a weak smile and "thank you." Then I watched him disappear into the sun-soaked morning.

My feet were so thick and heavy, I felt like an elephant lumbering through the savannah. When I got to the other side, I continued on to College Avenue and up to the university gates. I dragged myself past the Law building and the School of Business. I couldn't have felt more exhausted if I was climbing Mount Everest.

I'd only been to my brother's apartment a few times before, but I remembered exactly where to go. I climbed the stairs to the fourth floor and knocked on the door to his suite. There was no answer. I figured it wasn't even eight so it was a good bet he'd only been in bed a few hours. I pounded louder. Finally the door swung open.

"What's up?" his sleepy-eyed roommate asked.

"Is Joe here?"

"He's sleeping. His first class isn't 'til ten."

I pushed into the apartment my brother shared with three other students. When I looked around it became clear how all of them managed to fail enough courses that they were stuck in summer school.

"Tough life, starting the day at ten," I said.

Joe stumbled out of his room in grey boxer shorts.

"Anna! What's up?" He brightened when he saw me standing there.

"I was out for a walk and sort of lost track of where I was. I was hoping you could give me a ride home?"

I felt hollow standing there. Even seeing his puzzled expression didn't bring me back to reality the way it should have.

"You walked all the way here this morning?" he asked.

"Yeah. I couldn't sleep."

"Are you okay?" He stepped close to look into my eyes.

"I'm fine except for this blister on my foot."

I reached down to pull off my sandal as he scrutinized my eyes.

"Joe! I'm not on crack or anything. I just walked farther than I meant to. Can you please drive me home?"

He sized me up a minute longer, then said, "Sure. Let me grab my keys."

Then he disappeared down a narrow hall.

"Grab some shorts too!" I yelled after him.

Jamal was still standing by the door watching me. It made me feel creepy.

"What?" I finally asked so he'd say or do something — anything.

"Nothing. It's just, do you know how long it takes to walk across the city like that?"

I glanced at the clock in the kitchen.

"An hour and forty minutes. So what?"

He shrugged. "Seems a little odd this early in the morning."

"I like to get fresh air and it'll be too hot later."

He nodded, but I could tell he didn't buy it.

"You might try some walking shoes next time," he said.

I didn't get a chance to answer because Joe came out of his bedroom rattling his keys.

"Okay, let's hit the road before the traffic gets bad. You know what it's like getting across at this time of the day."

"See you, Jamal," I said, and followed Joe out the door.

I watched the top of Joe's head as we walked down the stairs. It took me a while to figure out what was different, then I realized he'd cut his hair, like, military short.

"That's a pretty drastic haircut. I haven't seen your ears since grade school."

"Yeah, it's cooler."

"I didn't know you were so worried about your street cred," I sniped.

"Temperature-wise," hc sniped back.

We always tease each other. It's our thing.

I followed him across the parking lot in silence, then sat down gratefully in the passenger seat of his beat-up Toyota. It smelled like something was decomposing under one of the seats, but I didn't complain.

"Everything okay at home?" he asked when he started the car.

"Pretty regular. I sort of had a fight with Dad this morning, but nothing serious."

"Otherwise everything's normal?"

"Yep. Dad went to LA this morning. Just one night."

"Mom's on mornings?"

I nodded.

He turned on the air conditioning and, after an initial blast of heat, I welcomed the cooler air. It chilled the sweat at my temples and made me shiver.

The traffic was backed up for three blocks before the bridge, which is pretty standard for a weekday when everyone is trying to get downtown for work. The closer we inched toward it, though, the more nauseous I felt.

"Hope you don't miss your class," I said.

"No worries. I'll make it back in time."

I leaned my head against the headrest, but the movement made me dizzy so I sat up straight again. Joe glanced over and I tried to smile.

"Maybe I'm getting the flu or something. Or it could be heat stroke," I offered. "I feel like I might throw up."

He looked at me sideways.

"Don't worry. I won't lose it in your car." I leaned a little closer to the air vent.

We were pulling onto the bridge when I reached up and locked the door. The urge to bolt from the car was overwhelming.

"You're not pregnant or something?" Joe asked. I could see him trying to puzzle through my unexpected visit.

"Not pregnant, not a druggie, not addicted to gambling. Maybe I'm just a little nervous about heights."

"But you can't even see how high you are from here."

"I still know."

"Then how'd you walk across in the first place?"

"It was foggy," I managed to squeak, even though I knew there was no logic in my answer.

When we got home, Sherlock met us at the door. His tail slapped the wall with the excitement of seeing both me and Joe arriving at once. Joe leaned down and rubbed his ears.

"Hey, Sherlock, how's the old boy?"

Sherlock dropped to the floor and let Joe rub his belly. For a dog who's supposed to be a guarding breed, he's a total coward. We have a lot in common that way.

Joe stood up and looked at me.

"Are you going to be okay by yourself?"

"Yeah, I'll be fine. I've got Sherlock."

"You want me to call Mom?"

"No. You know how she gets when she thinks you're getting sick. She'll be all over me like fleas on a stray dog."

Joe walked into the kitchen, opened the fridge, and drained the milk jug in one long gulp. He put the empty container back, then grabbed a hunk of kielbasa.

"That's disgusting," I said when he started gnawing on it.

Joe just laughed. "I won't have time for breakfast. Anyhow, I gotta run or I'll be late for my computer lab."

"Thanks for the ride."

"No worries." He kissed me on the cheek and slammed out the front door.

I wondered all morning if Joe would text Mom and tell her about me showing up at his dorm and needing a ride home, or if Dad managed to talk to her about our argument that morning. So when I heard her car pull into the driveway, I braced myself for a hundred questions. It must have slipped both their minds, though, because when Mom found me in my bedroom reading, she was cheerful.

"Hi, honey. How's your day going?"

"Good. I went for a walk this morning before it got too hot. Had a swim. Gisele and Aliya came over for a bit before lunch."

"Was Joe here?"

"Yeah, he stopped by. I think he picked up a piece of computer from his room."

"Stayed long enough to finish the milk?"

"He ate the rest of the kielbasa too."

Mom smiled and shook her head. "Figures. Anyhow, I'm going for a quick swim, then I thought we could make a pizza for dinner."

"Sounds good. I'll join you."

The thought of changing into my bathing suit seemed like a lot of effort, but I knew if I didn't go swimming, Mom would start to ask questions. And the last thing I wanted was her fussing over me.

I was floating on an air mattress, watching the sun turn my eyelids bright red and thinking about my walk across the bridge, when Mom slipped into the pool.

"That feels so good," she said and flipped onto her back.

I didn't answer, just continued to stare at the inside of my eyelids.

"Hey." Mom splashed water over me. "What's got you so preoccupied?"

I cracked one eyelid.

"Nuthin. Just enjoying the sun."

Mom climbed onto another air mattress and we floated together, but lost in separate thoughts.

I was thinking about how from the outside I look like a completely normal teenager. I live in a normal city, on a normal street in a very normal sidesplit house. We have a hedge around our backyard and a big maple tree in the front. Even my family is normal: two kids and two parents. I'm not ridiculed, bullied, or singled out in any way. I'm not fat or ugly and I don't have acne any worse than any other sixteen-year-old girl. I've never been beaten, neglected, or abused.

As I floated on the air mattress I thought about how someone on the outside would look at my life and think I was very average and middle-class. Some people, like Aliya, might even see me as privileged. The thing I was sure about, though, was that nobody would understand why I so badly wanted to stop existing. It's not that I wanted to kill myself. I just wanted a break from being me, which meant the thought of dying was never very far away. In fact, whenever I let myself think about it, I felt the torment fade away. I felt more at peace than usual. I know it's ironic. My whole life is one big irony. For instance, it feels like I've wanted to finish this life since I can remember. When I was a child, I wanted to hurry up and get old so I might finally fit in. I never felt like I belonged with other children, not even my brother. I didn't know how to play like the other kids. I didn't know when to laugh or how to be silly. I felt like a foreigner in my kindergarten class. It's like I knew from the beginning that I somehow ended up in the wrong place at the wrong time. I guess it's like ordering fettuccine alfredo at a restaurant and the waitress brings you a fruit salad instead. Even though it's perfectly edible, it just isn't what you want.

Mom kicked herself off the side of the pool and a few drops of water landed on me. I rolled over onto my stomach. Not surprisingly, my mind turned to my grandparents, which it did about every thirty minutes. Before they died I was resigned to the detached complacency that dragged on me every day. But after they were plowed into the river by a chronic drunk, I began to feel desperate, and after a few months of waking up to the same feeling of hopelessness every day, I started to get scared. I mean, you always hear people say they reached rock bottom before things started to get better. The thing that scared me most was that I might not have a rock bottom. I was afraid I'd keep going down into a deeper, darker hole.

# ALIYA

By grade nine I'd been the new kid so many times I'd stopped stressing about the first day of school. When I was little, I'd worry about what to wear and what to take in my lunch. I'd worry about if I should try and make friends right away or if I should wait and see who wanted to make friends with me. But by grade nine, I'd pretty much given up on any sort of plan. If I made a friend, I wouldn't have to eat alone, but if I didn't, well, I wasn't going to starve. But then I met Anna on my very first day at Bachman and everything turned around. I'd never met someone like Anna before. She was pretty and smart and she was exactly the type of artist I wanted to be — dedicated and focused.

Of course, my mom offered to go with me the first day of grade nine, but I straight up refused.

"Mom! This is like my sixth new school. I think I have it figured out by now."

She was getting ready to go to work and fussing over me at the same time.

"I can drive you, make sure you get to your homeroom okay. This one's a lot bigger than any of your other schools. What if you get lost?"

"I'll stop at the office and get directions. I can handle it. Stop worrying. You're already late for work."

"I'm allowed to be late now and then. This is a big day for you. Your first day of high school. I'm still so proud you got accepted." She was starting to get that nostalgic look on her face which meant I either had to get her out of the apartment or get out myself before the tears started.

"I'll be fine," I insisted, and picked up my book bag.

"But you have to catch two buses. Remember to get a transfer from the driver."

"I've been riding the city buses my whole life. I won't forget."

"But now you'll be alone. And it's not you I'm worried about. I trust you. It's everyone else you have to watch out for."

"Okay, really, Mom! I love you but you have to chill. I'm almost fifteen."

I gave her a reassuring hug and kiss, then slipped out the door. I knew she was standing in the hallway, watching me walk toward the elevator, but I refused to turn around.

"Do you have your cellphone?" she called out.

I waved it in the air above my head but continued walking.

"Call if you need anything," she called again.

The elevator opened and I jumped in. Thankfully it was empty.

I saw Anna get on my second bus but I had no idea who she was or that we were headed to the same school. Still, I noticed her right away. It would be hard not to notice Anna for a few reasons. First, she's beautiful, but not in an obvious self-conscious sort of way. When she walks in the room everyone turns to look, even the girls. Second, she has a mysterious quality about her. It's like she's distracted and you want to know what's got her attention. I'm sure most guys wish they were the distraction, but she barely seems to notice guys. And finally, it's hard not to notice someone carrying a big black case.

Anyhow, she climbed on the bus and all the men followed her down the aisle with their eyes. Most of the women did too. Then she sat down across from me and stared out the window. She sat so still she looked like a painting. I ached to sketch her, but I didn't want her to think I was stalking her or something. Still, I watched her out of the corner of my eye. Now don't get me wrong, I'm not into girls. I LIKE guys. But Anna had me intrigued from the start. When we stood up at the same time and got off the bus together, I couldn't hold back.

"Do you go to Bachman?" I asked her as soon as we both landed on the sidewalk.

She continued and I walked a little faster than I normally would to keep up.

She nodded.

"It's my first day," she said. When she turned to face me, I almost fell into her eyes.

"Really? Me too. I'm starting in the visual arts program. What about you?"

"Same." She smiled.

I nodded at the case in her hand. "What's that?"

"I like to use my own art supplies," she explained.

"Oh. I assumed it was a saxophone or something."

She laughed and said something like, "No, nothing musical. I'm completely tone deaf. I can't even sing 'Happy Birthday.'"

We made small talk as we walked the last block to school and it felt like we'd been friends forever. She asked which school I'd gone to and stopped walking when I listed them all on my fingers.

"You've been to five schools?" she asked like she couldn't wrap her head around the thought of changing schools so often.

"We move around a lot. My mom hates to commute, so when she gets a new job, we move."

"What about your dad?"

"It's just me and my mom."

I didn't have to ask where Anna lived. I saw where she got on the bus and I wasn't surprised she came from one of the rich neighbourhoods, one of those areas with wide lawns and big trees, where the houses are set way back off the street and the backyards have garden sheds the size of my bedroom. She was dressed like she was loaded, but she didn't once glance at the holes in my high tops or seem to notice the front of my book bag was pinned together.

That was it, from that moment on Anna and I were best friends. We had most of our classes together and the same lunch period so it was easy to hang out and sit at the same table in the cafeteria. Because the school draws kids from all over the city, neither of us knew any of our other classmates. But it turned out Anna knew a girl, Mariam, from her middle school and I knew Kyle from my junior high. Mariam and Kyle were both in the performing arts stream so we immediately formed a group. That meant there was always someone to hang out with. I was so happy, I didn't even mind that Kyle was interested in Anna from the very beginning.

"Who's that girl you were talking to this morning?" Kyle asked me the first morning. Somehow he'd tracked me down at my locker between classes.

"Kyle!" I said. "I didn't know you were coming here?"

"I got accepted late." He watched some girls walk past. "Someone dropped out and I was on the waiting list."

"Sweet." We bumped fists. "It's going to be a wicked year."

"So who was that girl?" he asked again.

"Her name's Anna. I just met her today. She's in visual arts with me."

"Can you introduce us?" He looked so pathetic I didn't have the heart to tease him.

"I guess. I mean, I hardly know her but if you're both standing beside me of course I'm going to introduce you to each other."

"Thanks." He smiled like I'd just told him she thought he was hot.

"How'd you find me, anyway?" I shut my locker and started walking to my next class. I was pretty sure I was going in the right direction.

"I asked at the office and they gave me your locker number. I came between periods one and two, but I missed you."

"What? Are you like stalking me or something?" I laughed.

He shook his head and looked worried, like I was going to get the wrong impression about our friendship.

"Just kidding," I said. "Both my morning classes are in the art wing so I hung with Anna. She showed me her paintbrushes. Sable. Her grandmother gave them to her or something."

"Just don't forget to introduce us. Maybe tomorrow at lunch?" he suggested hopefully.

"Chill, Frozone."

By Thanksgiving, Kyle was discouraged. No matter what he did to get Anna to notice him she never seemed to pick up on it. She talked to him the same as she talked to the rest of us, but she never singled him out and I think it drove him crazy. I don't think Kyle ever had to work so hard to get a girl's attention.

He found me on Facebook that long weekend. Even before he mentioned her name I knew where he was headed. I mean, sure we were friends in junior high but it wasn't like we spent our weekends together. It wasn't like we chatted every night.

"Do you think she likes me?" he wrote eventually, after he'd steered the conversation like a race car driver to end up at her.

"I'm sure she likes you."

"I mean, do you think she LIKE likes me?"

"Dunno. Hard to tell with her. I think your best bet is to play it cool," I wrote, even though it stung a little. I mean, this is Kyle we're talking about and he's basically smokin' hot.

"Put in a good word for me if you get a chance."

"I'll do my best :o)"

By December I was used to the situation. Kyle secretly drooled over Anna and she pretended not to notice, or maybe it's not that she was pretending, but something was holding her back even though I was pretty sure she liked him too. I mean, who wouldn't? Whenever I asked her about him, she changed the subject. That's when I knew that even though we spent so much time together, she wasn't one for sharing all her secrets. And I was okay with that. I mean, there was a lot I hadn't told her either. I hadn't told her about all the crappy years I spent at school without any friends, or that my mom's sister had committed suicide in high school, which meant my mom was basically an overprotective nutbar.

Then, just before Christmas, Anna's grandparents got in that accident and it was tough on her. I mean, she wasn't a basket case or anything. She didn't miss much school and she didn't come to class with red swollen eyes. She didn't go out and party away her sadness or mouth off to the teachers because she had an excuse to be in a crap mood. She just seemed more distant. Sometimes it felt like I was more upset about her grandparents than she was. I'd only met them a few times, but they were really cool for old people, especially her grandmother. I went sketching with Anna and Granny a few times during the fall of grade nine. We went down into the ravine by the west branch of the river, where, like Granny used to say, "the sound of the water lets you get lost in your work."

Anyhow, after her grandparents were killed, Anna changed a bit. I know it's completely understandable considering the circumstances, but instead of wanting to hang out in the cafeteria at lunch, she started going to the art room to paint. It just about drove Kyle mad that she was always sneaking off. It sort of bugged me too. I mean, I know she loves to paint and I totally envy her dedication. But by grade ten, painting had taken over her life, especially the creepy bridge painting that Kyle fell in love with, the one Mrs. Galloway chose for the student exhibit. Normally it's only the grade twelve students who get their art chosen. But Anna painted a picture of the West River Viaduct that was so remarkable, I knew before it was even finished it would be chosen.

The viaduct is the biggest landmark around. There's a whole bunch of history to it too. Apparently seventy-seven workers died in the early 1900s while they were building it, so there are all sorts of legends and myths about the souls of the dead luring people to jump off. It's the kind of thing kids talk about at parties, especially around Halloween. I think it's a bunch of crap, but the painting was so haunting it almost made me believe the stories. I think Anna is the only person who can turn something as normal as a bridge into a beautiful piece of art.

When Kyle found out about the exhibit, he begged me to take him. We both knew Anna would tell him not to come if he said he wanted to go, but it would seem normal if he came with me. So, of course, being the good friend I am to them both, I agreed to meet him ahead of time and walk in together. We arranged to meet at the Starbucks down the street and have a quick Frappuccino. When I arrived, he was already sitting there with two iced drinks sweating rings of condensation onto the table. He was acting edgy and weird.

"What's up with you?" I asked him finally. "You're acting suspicious, like you're packing a gun or something."

"Yeah, right," he grunted. "I'm just nervous."

"About going to the art exhibit?"

"No. I made up my mind to ask her out. Once and for all. I've waited long enough. I just have to know if she likes me or not." He fidgeted with his cellphone as he spoke.

"You're going to ask her, like, on a date?" Even though they'd been friends almost two years, I couldn't imagine Kyle and Anna alone together at a movie or eating at a restaurant. It seemed too weird.

"Maybe just for coffee to start. Tonight after the show or something."

"You're going to ditch me?"

He looked at me and rolled his eyes. It was obvious he wasn't in the mood for me to be difficult.

Anna's picture was hanging on the wall in the front entrance to the student gallery. Her painting could be in the city gallery, it's that good. Even from outside the door, I saw it and felt chills go up my back. She painted it in early morning, with mist rising up from the river and muted sunlight in the background. There's a single girl standing in the middle of the bridge, her head turned toward the bank of the ravine, looking off in the distance.

When we first arrived, Kyle and I did a lap of the gallery together. The place was packed so it took us a while to find Anna. Groups of students and teachers were huddled around talking about use of colour and how this painting used a modernist technique and that one had an eighteenth-century quality. Within ten minutes Kyle was complaining.

"I feel totally out of place here. All I know about a picture is if I like it or not."

"We come to your dance recitals," I pointed out.

"That's different. It's a show. It's entertaining."

"This is a show," I countered.

We found Anna tucked away in a corner. It looked like she didn't want to be there at all, even though everyone kept going over to tell her how wonderful her painting was and how it evoked so much emotion. She looked uncomfortable and examined the floor. It's not that she's shy. When you get to know her she's funny. But maybe she doesn't like attention the way some kids in the performance stream do. Take Kyle, for instance, he loves being in front of an audience, but I guess not everyone's like him.

When Anna was finally alone, we walked over to where she was standing beside a pillar and said hi. Then Kyle gave me the look to let me know it would be a good time to disappear so I moved a few feet away.

"It looks like your painting is the star of the show," Kyle said to her.

I hung on the edge of the conversation.

She looked up, surprised to see him, but maybe a little bit pleased.

"I didn't expect to see you here," she said as she rubbed her thumb along her cheekbone. Kyle just about melts when she does that.

"It's an amazing painting. I know I've seen it, I dunno, come to life, but it's even better now that it's done."

I bit my tongue when Kyle said that. It was an idiotic comment, but Anna didn't seem to notice.

She mumbled, "Thanks."

"I know this sounds crazy, but it almost looks alive — it's so realistic."

I pretended to be looking at one of the grade twelve sculptures.

"It's just a bridge. I don't even know why I painted it," Anna said.

"Well it's never going to be just a bridge to me anymore."

Tragically, I think he really did say something like that. Normally Kyle is pretty good at chatting up girls, but when it comes to Anna he sort of loses his cool. Anna looked away.

"I mean, I wish I could paint half as well as you. I can't even draw stick people," he said, trying to recover.

"I wish I could dance without tripping over one of my three left feet." She turned back toward him.

I laughed to myself. I couldn't help it. She has the best timing and delivery. I think she almost smiled, or was about to smile, until someone came over and started talking about her painting again. Then Kyle shuffled over near me and said he was ready to go.

"What do you mean you want to go? You didn't ask her out yet?"

"I can't. I feel stupid standing here. You coming or not?"

I followed him out of the school to help him lick his wounds, even though I knew it was going to be a long night.

# ANNA'S MOM

I knew Anna had a gift by the time she was three. When other kids were scribbling stick figures, she was shading in noses and eye sockets. When other kids were playing house and dress-up she would be in the corner at a Little Tykes easel drawing the plastic animals. She had no patience for other kids' frivolous play and especially not their artwork. One day at playgroup, when she wasn't yet four, she tried to explain what one of the other girls had done wrong.

"Cats don't have legs like sticks," she said, pointing to the girl's picture.

"My cat does," the little redhead replied.

"No he doesn't. How can he walk without feet?"

The girl picked up her paintbrush and drew a circle at the bottom of each stick leg.

"Cat feet aren't round like that," Anna insisted.

I was talking to another mother across the room and only partly paying attention.

"My cat does," the little redhead said.

"He does not! That's impossible." Anna took her own paintbrush and started drawing a proper outline around the cat

The little redheaded girl started screaming.

"She's wrecking my picture. Anna's wrecking my picture!"

That's when I ran over to settle the commotion.

"Anna, sweetheart, you can't paint on Jenna's picture like that." I steered her back to her own easel.

"I was just trying to fix it for her. She did it all wrong. You ask Granny. It's okay that it's blue but it can't be made of sticks." Anna was exasperated.

"Not everyone can draw like you," I said quietly, trying to calm her down.

"They could if they tried. You just have to draw what you see and I never seed a cat that had feet like balls."

She slipped a new sheet of paper onto her easel and started painting a cat. She worked quickly, feverishly, and when she was finished she pulled it down and took it over to the red-headed girl.

"This is what a cat looks like," Anna said and shoved it in her face.

The girl's mother looked up at me and scowled. "Did you paint that?" she asked me.

I shook my head apologetically. "I'm sorry. Anna takes her artwork very seriously."

The mother sized me up. "Are you trying to tell me your three-year-old daughter painted that?"

I knew it would seem impossible to a stranger, but I was already used to Anna's talent by then. "Yes, she seems to have a gift for drawing. But she doesn't get it from me. I'm still at stick figures too." I laughed, trying to lighten the tension.

The woman refused to smile. She pulled her daughter over to the giant building blocks and started on a castle.

"Can we go home now?" Anna said after that. "I want to use the watercolours Granny gave me. The water paints here are all orange. Someone mixed the colours together."

I took Anna home and never went back to playgroup again. Instead, my mother came over three mornings a week to give her art lessons. My mother had been an artist. She wasn't professional, but when she was around she was forever sketching, painting, and taking classes. When I was a child we never ate in our dining room because it was stacked with half-finished canvases and our kitchen sink was usually full of dirty paintbrushes. I didn't inherit any artistic talent, so I was happy to see the art gene skipped to the next generation. My mother was pleased too. Or maybe she wasn't so much pleased as relieved. She'd been watching for it in Joe, but he was always more interested in building Lego inventions than drawing. When Anna came along, it was like a dream come true for my mother. Finally she had someone she could mentor, someone with real talent. In fact, she always said Anna had more natural ability than she ever did.

To be perfectly honest, I felt left out when my mother and Anna were together. Once Anna started going to school, the art lessons shifted to the weekends. A couple times a month, as long as it wasn't raining, they'd go on drawing expeditions down along the river where there were few people to interrupt them. When Anna was little, I'd tag along with a book and a backpack full of snacks and wait for them to take a break from sketching so we could all talk. But they used their breaks to look at their work, to talk about it, to make suggestions on how to improve the composition or the perspective. They'd inhale the juice boxes and cookies I'd brought without even noticing I was there, then start on another picture. By the time she was ten, Anna was sketching textbook-quality trees and flowers, insects and birds. By the time she was twelve, I just handed my mother the backpack and told them to be back before dinner. I got tired of being in the way.

Eventually, Anna met a friend with an interest in art. It was a relief for me to see her with someone her own age and with the same level of talent. It made her seem less precocious. She'd always had friends to play with and birthday parties to go to, but I worried that because they didn't understand her need to paint and draw, she never really connected with her classmates. Then she got accepted to the arts high school and I was sure she'd find kids like her who spent all their spare time sketching and painting. In fact, she met Aliya on her first day at Bachman. I'd never seen her so excited before.

"How was school?" I asked when I got home. Anna was in her bedroom, on her laptop, which was her second favourite preoccupation next to drawing. I'd wondered all day how she was making out and resisted, more than once, calling to check on her.

"Good," she said without looking up. "Our painting teacher, Mrs. Galloway, has a painting in the gallery downtown and I met this really cool girl, Aliya, in my class. She's on the same bus as me and everything. She's really talented. You should see how well she can draw people's faces. I'm hopeless with portraits, but look, she drew this at lunch in the cafeteria."

Anna pulled a sheet of paper out of her backpack and fluttered it at me. I stepped forward and took it. It was stunning. She'd drawn Anna perfectly, with a questioning look in her eyes that I recognized but had never been able to understand.

"She drew this over lunch?"

"Yep. And she knows a guy in the performance stream who is in the same modern dance class as Mariam. It's such a sweet school."

"I'm glad you had a good first day. Maybe you can have Aliya over sometime," I suggested.

"She's going to come drawing this weekend with Granny and me. She said she needs more practice with plants and you know that's Granny's specialty."

Anna and my mom were like part of the same person. I think Anna had a hard time seeing where she ended and my mother began. I've never seen anything like it, two people so similar. Whereas my mother always mystified me, Anna could tell what she was thinking before she even spoke. It took effort on my part, but by the time Anna became a teenager I'd learned to accept and even be grateful for their relationship. If she wasn't confiding in me, at least I knew she was talking to someone. My mom, of course, passed along things she thought I should know: what boy Anna liked in her class, what mean thing one of her friends said, the intolerable things I said and did. So for years, I knew my daughter through my mother and, of course, I saw my mother through Anna's eyes. Sometimes it was a hard pill to swallow, especially considering the relationship I had with my mother was inconsistent and strained much of my childhood and teenage years, but their connection kept me tethered to them both. Then I lost my mother, both parents just before Christmas, and I lost part of my connection to Anna too.

The only way to describe what it felt like to lose both parents at once is blindsided. It's impossible to piece together my memories of the day and it's sickening how the morning seemed so slow and deliberate until the police arrived. After that my brain short-circuited and I can't recall what happened first or second. My husband insists I called him to come home while the police were still at the house and yet I remember him being away on a business trip until the next day. I was in that limbo for hours it seemed, until I remembered Anna and Joe. I knew they were both going to be devastated. I didn't think I could face them with the news, but there wasn't much choice.

Joe's school was closer, so he got home first, and as soon as I saw him, I saw the fear in his eyes.

"Anna?" he asked, when he found me huddled in bed crying.

"She's not home yet," I managed to wail. "Granny and Gramps were in an accident. They've both been killed."

Joe's knees buckled and he sank to the floor. I knew I should go to him but I couldn't move.

"I should have called you." It was the only thought I could form until I heard the front door open.

"Mom?" Anna called from the living room. She wouldn't know to look in the bedroom for me.

"Joe?" she called out again.

The house was too quiet, I realized too late. She knew something was wrong right away.

Everyone deals with tragedy differently, I know that, but Anna's reaction was almost eerie. She came into the bedroom and looked at Joe crying on the floor, then at me sobbing on the bed. I'd been crying for hours by then and my face must have been puffy and unrecognizable. Joe had his face buried in his knees. She didn't speak a word but waited at the doorway. I wanted to say something, anything, but my throat was strangled with grief. Finally

Joe took one long shuddering sob and said: "Granny and Gramps were in a car accident."

Anna stepped into the room and sat quietly on the end of my bed. Her cheeks were still red from being outside in the cold.

"Are they okay?" she asked.

"No, sweetheart. They died." I choked on the last word.

"How?"

"Their car went into the river."

"They drowned?"

I nodded and gasped.

She sat on the end of the bed with her head down. She didn't cry or move. I wasn't even sure she was breathing. When my husband came home finally, she looked at him and scowled.

"Where have you been?" she asked.

"With the police," he stammered.

It was news to me.

Anna handled their deaths remarkably well. She was stoic and proper, but I was a blubbering mess for months. I had so many of my own deep-rooted issues to work through, including the immobilizing anger at the drunk who slammed into their car one nondescript Thursday morning, that I barely had the energy to worry about anything or anyone else. I don't think we went through with any of our Christmas traditions. I was too busy progressing through the stages of grief like the perfect student: denial, anger, bargaining, depression.

I still haven't moved on to acceptance yet. I can't because I haven't forgiven my mother for putting her art ahead of me. And then there were those unexplained absences, months at a time when she was mysteriously gone without an explanation.

I'm still digging through a closet of dusty skeletons to find out what that was all about.

When I finally recovered a little, after about six months when the shock at least lifted, I looked to Anna for signs of her suffering, but she never missed a beat. I watched her school grades for the slightest fluctuation, but nothing. She kept bringing home As and Bs in her academic courses and straight As in her art classes. I watched for her to lose interest in her art, but that didn't happen either. If anything she became even more dedicated. I watched to see if she would pull away from us or her friends. But nothing of the sort happened. Her girlfriends were remarkably supportive and she seemed secure in their friendships. I was so relieved that she was going to be okay. I took pride in her strength. I assumed it was because she was young that she handled what I couldn't, that she was coping so well because kids adapt without thinking. I was almost glad she didn't have to lose them when she was an adult like me, when the struggle would last longer and cut deeper.

Then came the bridge painting that made it into the year-end exhibit. Her teacher called even before Anna finished painting it.

"It's a stunning piece of work, simply remarkable. I've never had a student with so much talent. You should be proud of her. But it's very dark," Mrs. Galloway confessed. "Is Anna going through anything difficult at home?"

Even though I'd been waiting for it, the suggestion staggered me.

"Her grandparents were killed in a car accident last year, but she seems to be doing fine. All her marks are good, she has friends, she talks to her father and me all the time."

"I just wanted to touch base to be sure. Sometimes I see things in my students' work that concern me and I like to follow up."

For days after the phone call I thought about Anna and my parents' accident. I couldn't tie any real changes in Anna's behaviour to their deaths so I made an effort to put it out of my mind. I kept telling myself that everyone handles grief in their own way. It was the only explanation that made any sense to me.

We didn't see the painting until the opening night of the art show. Anna hadn't made too much out of it being chosen, but when we looked around we saw that all the other pieces were by grade twelve students and Anna's was by far the most outstanding. We listened to other parents remark on the fact that Anna was only in grade ten. I beamed the entire night, but Anna seemed unsure of herself for the first time ever. When I asked her about it on the drive home she said, "I don't like being singled out. I don't want the other students to, you know, resent me or anything."

It seemed like a very mature observation.

I loved the painting. It was dark, yes, but it was so realistic it took my breath away. I wanted to frame it and show it off, but I didn't tell Anna. I wanted to surprise her. When she told me she'd given it to her teacher, I was heartbroken. I didn't let on how I felt because I didn't want her to feel bad. But the disappointment stayed with me most of the summer and then it was replaced by the confusion that came with the new school year.

It was only the second week of grade eleven when the principal called to tell me Anna had skipped a class. I didn't think it was possible and said there must have been some sort of mistake. I trusted Anna. She'd always been a responsible kid. Even when she was in the primary grades she was level-headed and honest. But when I called her cellphone and she didn't pick up, I started to worry. I immediately assumed the worst — that she'd been in an accident. Then I talked myself down to the possibility she was just feeling sick. I called the house but there was no answer there either. That's when I decided to leave work early and go home. While I drove, all sorts of terrifying thoughts went through my head and I prayed she'd just skipped class to hang out with her friends. By the time I got home I didn't care what her reason was for missing class, I just wanted to know she was safe. But she wasn't at home and it was only one-thirty. I realized she wouldn't get home for at least another two hours.

My initial instinct was to sit on the front lawn and wait, but even to me that seemed unbalanced. So I decided to put myself to work trimming the rose bushes at the side of the house. It had been too long since they'd had any real attention and I'd been meaning to rescue them for weeks. I was in the basement looking for the garden shears when I discovered Anna's bridge painting wrapped in plastic and tucked behind an old dresser. Questions landed like bombs around me: Why was it hidden down there? Why did she want to hide it? Why had she lied to us? What else had she lied about?

I wasn't mad so much as mystified about why she'd hidden the painting in the first place. It was one more thing I had to figure out, so I hauled the painting upstairs, unwrapped it, and set it by the front door. I hoped when she saw it her expression would give me some answers, even if she wouldn't.

It was almost dinner by the time she got home. By then all the gardens were in order and I was sitting on the stairs petting Sherlock. When she walked inside I said, "The school called and said you missed period three. I thought maybe you were sick."

"I'm fine," she said but she looked annoyed to see me there beside her painting. It was just a quick flicker in her eyes, but I saw it.

"Are you sure?"

"I didn't mean to. I was working on a sculpture and lost track of time."

"I knew there must have been a good explanation. But I was worried. You didn't answer your phone."

She pulled her cellphone out of her pocket and rolled her eyes. "Crap, I forgot to turn it on after first period. Mrs. Galloway doesn't let us have them on in class."

"Don't let it become a habit. Your academic classes are just as important as your art classes."

"I know. I'll be more careful from now on."

"Now about this painting," I said in what I hoped was a lighter tone. "I thought you said you gave it to Mrs. Galloway?"

"I just didn't want you to make a big deal of it. I don't think it's that great."

"But it's fantastic! I hope you don't mind but I want to hang it in the dining room. I'm going to take it and get it framed."

"Whatever," she said and tried to step past me to go up the stairs.

"Hey."

She turned back but didn't look at me.

"Is everything okay? I mean, you seem a little distracted lately. Is there something I should know about?"

"Everything's fine. I just don't like that painting as much as everyone else does. I'm sure I have a better painting in me somewhere."

"I'm sure you do too. So everything's okay?"

She nodded.

"No troubles with your friends?"

"I'm fine."

"Any troubles with a boy?"

"No. I'm fine. I'm sorry I worried you. I really just got caught up in my sculpture."

"You'll talk to me if you have a problem?"

"I promise," she said and headed up to her room.

My husband brought me to my senses later that evening when he saw the painting in the entrance.

"I thought she gave that away?" he said.

I was leaning against the wall beside it.

"I thought so too until I found it downstairs behind Joe's old dresser."

"Odd."

Men can be so understated.

"Did she say why she put it down there?"

"She said she didn't like it."

"So what's it doing here?"

"I'm going to get it framed and hang it in the dining room."

He raised his eyebrows at me. "Why do you want to do that if she doesn't like it?"

"Because it's a beautiful picture and I want to show it off. I think Mom would have loved it."

I stopped talking when he put his fingers to his temples and said in a quiet voice, "Oh my God." The colour drained out of his face. I looked around to see what was wrong.

"I just got it," he said.

"Got what?"

"What it's a picture of."

"What do you mean?"

"Look at the girl. Which way is she facing?"

I looked at the angle of the river, at the skyline beyond the bridge. I closed my eyes and tried to put myself there.

"Southwest, I guess."

"And what's southwest of the West River Viaduct?" he prompted.

"Downtown."

"And what connects downtown to the viaduct?"

"River Road."

The thoughts were slow to form in my mind. I felt the shock before I actually made a conscious connection in my mind. Then I gasped out loud. The girl on the bridge was looking across the ravine to where my parents' car had been forced off the road and plunged into the river.

# ANNA

By some miracle the bridge stopped haunting me, even though the urge to escape living didn't. If anything, I was deeper down the hole and the beam of light shining in on me was getting smaller and dimmer. How could I not feel worse? What seemed like the perfect ending was beyond my grasp. I might not have been so worried, but I saw a girl on a talk show that same week. She had no legs and only one arm. She'd lost her limbs and almost her life when she'd lain on the subway tracks and waited to be crushed to death. Something went wrong. She said a guardian angel was protecting her, and, although her body was terribly mangled, she was left alive. She never lost consciousness, even after the subway passed and she saw her leg lying a few feet down the tracks. She was in the hospital the better part of two years, had to have multiple surgeries, skin grafts, and extensive physiotherapy. But she said she's never been so full of life, so full of happiness. She said she finally has a sense about the meaning of life. When someone asked her why she wanted to kill herself in the first place, she said she'd wanted to escape the memories of her childhood.

That made me feel like a fraud because I don't have a good reason, not one I can explain anyway. Aliya always tells me I have the perfect life, but that just makes me feel double defective because I should be grateful and I'm not, or I can't be. I'm not sure which it is.

If there's one thing I know without a doubt, it's that I don't want to end up like that girl. I'd rather suffer through my aimless life for another seventy years than be the object of pity and speculation. I couldn't imagine facing my friends after failing, especially if I went and lost half my body. I know getting mangled wouldn't help me find a purpose or bring a smile to my face. But I'm happy for her, I guess. I mean, I don't resent her happiness just because it escapes me. Maybe if I did hold a grudge, maybe if I did get mad, maybe then I'd feel more alive than I do right now. Feeling anger or hate would at least be feeling something. Sometimes I check my own pulse, just to convince myself I haven't slipped away into the blackness yet.

Anyhow, I figured that girl's mistake was hanging her legs over the metal track and that if she'd just stood to face the subway train, she'd have been crushed to death the way she intended. Either that or she would have been smashed into a million bits. Whatever. The end result would be being dead.

Then it happened and an idea got stuck in my brain again. It repeated itself over and over, a persistent nagging that told me there was no harm in going to look. There aren't any subways in our city or any train tracks near my house, but there's a busy highway where transport trucks speed past and my brain told me it made sense to check it out, in an academic sort of way, to see if it was possible for a person to get in front of a speeding truck without screwing it up

Luckily, the expressway that circles the perimeter of the city runs two blocks behind my school. So one day in early September I planned to go off property for lunch. I packed a sandwich and a drink. I even threw in a dessert, just to make the outing legitimate. I was at my locker, putting the lunch bag in my backpack, when Mariam found me.

"What are you doing for lunch?" she asked when she saw me getting ready to go out.

"I felt like getting away for a while, you know."

"Where to?"

"I dunno. Just for walk around. Maybe find a sunny place to sit and eat."

"But they're starting intramural volleyball today."

I knew I should say something like "sweet," but all I could force myself to say was: "Oh yeah? Good luck."

"You're not signing up?"

"My wrist is still bothering me from when I fractured it last year. Mom and Dad want me to give it a rest this fall."

"I didn't know you hurt your wrist?"

"Yeah, I slipped on a rock one weekend down by the river. I didn't need a cast but it still hurts," I lied.

"But I don't want to go all by myself."

"Aliya will be there too. You won't be alone."

"But it won't be the same without you."

"I'll come to cheer you on," I said with as much sincerity as I could fake.

"You're so sweet!" Mariam said and wrapped me in a quick hug. Then she bounced off down the hall. Mariam has enough energy for three volleyball teams. I don't understand how one person can contain so much life. I could live a week off the few bits of DNA she leaves on a cafeteria chair.

I walked out of the school and down the street. I heard the traffic whining on the highway as soon as I turned the corner. There were other kids on the street too. Some were heading to restaurants for lunch and others to their homes. I live thirty minutes away by bus so it isn't possible to go home and back in one lunch hour.

The sun was out and the air warm for September. It felt like the middle of summer and I was hot in my jeans. Still, I walked on and listened as the roar of the highway traffic grew steadily louder. I found a path that led between two rows of houses and stopped at the bank overlooking the highway. I scrambled over the wooden fence and found a few small trees to sit under.

I unwrapped my sandwich and chewed slowly. It tasted like paper, but I swallowed each bite with a swig of juice. Eighteen wheelers ripped past so fast I could feel the breeze on my face. Trucks and cars, vans and motorbikes — they all whizzed past and I sat unnoticed. I imagined a truck plowing over 120 pounds of flesh, like a giant raccoon that wandered onto the highway by accident. The thought of so much blood made my stomach clench and I took a gulp of air.

Next I thought about Kyle and the way he'd come to the art exhibit with Aliya. They spent so much time together I sometimes I thought they were, like, a couple. But then sometimes it seemed Kyle liked me. That was the impression I got at the art exhibit anyway. I thought he had something he wanted to say, until someone came along and started to talk about natural-fibre brushes compared to nylon fibres. That's when Kyle took off. I don't think he has much patience for talking art supplies. What *would Kyle think if I was dead?* I wondered. *Would he even care? Would he crumple to the floor and cry the way Joe did when my grandparents were killed? Would he forget to eat or shower for months on end, the way my mother did?* I seriously doubted it, but part of me thought he'd be pretty shaken up. I mean, hey, I'd be shaken up if one of my friends died. I was when Granny died, that's for sure.

I don't know how long I sat there watching the traffic. I was almost in a trance when I noticed someone beside me. It was a man wearing an orange and yellow vest and carrying a garbage bag. He had a long pointed stick in one hand.

"Odd place to eat your lunch," he said.

*Not another jogger*, I thought before I turned to see who was talking.

"I guess." I crumpled my sandwich wrapper into a ball. "I'm counting cars for a math project. Probability. It's hard to explain."

As usual I was impressed with my ability to think fast and deliver a perfectly believable lie.

"Well, I appreciate you not littering." He nodded at the wad of plastic wrap clenched in my hand. He had a crooked smirk on his face, like he was waiting for me to say something funny in return.

"No problem. I hate when people litter." That part wasn't a lie.

"You and me both," he said and stabbed at a candy bar wrapper with his stick.

I watched him for a minute and he started to whistle. It surprised me because I expected him to be annoyed about having to pick up other people's garbage.

"Do you do that every day?" I asked.

He was circling around me, adding candy bar wrappers and coffee cups to his bag of trash. I hadn't even noticed I was sitting amongst so much litter.

"Most days." He smiled. "Some days they have me cutting grass. Or plowing snow in the winter."

I was stunned. Here this poor guy was out picking up garbage and whistling show tunes at the same time and it didn't look like he had the slightest urge to throw himself in front of a speeding truck. In fact, he seemed oddly happy.

"What did you say you were doing here again?" he asked.

"Math project. Statistics."

"Statistics and probability at the same time? They sure teach complicated math these days."

"I know. It's just about killing me."

I winced at my choice of words and he lowered his eyes at me.

"Stick in school is all I can say. Especially if you don't want to find yourself picking up garbage like me." He laughed and stepped into the ditch. A transport truck roared past and his ball cap tumbled off his head. He stooped down and picked it up.

He turned and called to me, "You better do your math project up the bank a bit. This is restricted access down here. That's why they put that fence up. They don't want people and pets wandering out onto the highway and getting killed."

"Good point." I picked up my backpack and said, "See you later."

I climbed the steep embankment toward the fence. Before I hoisted myself over, I turned and watched the garbage man against the backdrop of speeding vehicles.

It was a lot harder getting over the fence from the highway side because the ground was lower. I had to try twice before I could pull myself high enough to rest my shoulders over the top. Then I kicked against the wooden slats with my feet. I landed back on the sidewalk with a thump.

"Anna?"

Without even seeing who had spoken, I recognized Kyle's voice and my heart did a series of tumbles.

"Hey, Kyle," I said as cheerfully as I could manage, while my mind raced with possible explanations. Inside though, I was panicking.

"What were you doing down there?"

I barely heard the question I was thinking so hard, but it didn't matter. There was only one question he could be asking.

"Oh. Uh, my brother moved last weekend and lost a box of stuff off the truck. I thought maybe that guy might have seen it." The lie dissolved on my tongue like a spoonful of ice cream.

Kyle looked over the fence at the man picking up garbage and nodded.

"What are you doing here?" I asked quickly before he could ask another question.

"I have period-three lunch and I live down the street."

I followed his gaze to the new subdivision behind me, the kind where the houses are packed in like kernels of corn on a cob.

We stepped into rhythm together on our way back to school.

"Don't you have period-two lunch this term?"

"Yeah. Why?"

He pulled a cellphone from his pocket and checked the time.

"You're late," he said.

"Crap. I must have lost track of time."

"On the side of the highway?"

"Yeah, I was thinking about a new painting."

Kyle looked down at the highway again, then at the overpass in the distance. He probably thought I was some sort of bridge-obsessed freak.

"Either way, you shouldn't go down there, you know. Especially at night. My cousin was hitchhiking along a highway at night and a truck hit him. The driver didn't even know he'd killed someone, thought he'd hit some garbage on the road. It wasn't until he got home and saw the blood that he called the police and they found my cousin's body in the ditch. He probably didn't even see it coming."

"Oh God, I'm sorry to hear that," I said.

"I was only a baby when it happened. But at least he didn't cause a huge pile up," Kyle continued. "I mean, if the driver had seen him and swerved, it could have killed a whole bunch of people."

"That would have been pretty awful."

When we got to school we said goodbye and headed in different directions. I walked to my locker and thought again about the busy highway. The idea that a desperate person could cause an accident and kill innocent people didn't sit well with me. If there was a God and I had to meet him, explain to him why I took my own life, I sure didn't want to have to be responsible for any other lives. I mean, just because I wanted to die didn't mean I wanted anyone else to get hurt. I still had a conscience. I wasn't a total sketch.

I was just closing my locker when Aliya walked up.

"Did you go out for volleyball?" I asked.

"They ended up cancelling intramurals today. The gym is set up for an assembly. What happened to you, anyway? You missed class."

"Just walked around and stuff. Lost track of time. I hope they don't call Mom. She'll freak."

"Was Kyle enjoying the nice weather too?" Aliya threw back her head and laughed, then leaned close to me and started singing, "Anna and Kyle, sitting in a tree. K-i-s-s-i-n-g."

"Whatever. I just ran into him." I kept my cool, but my hands started to sweat. I was afraid my lies were about to collide.

When I got home after school and saw Mom's car was already in the driveway, I knew I was in for it. But when I walked in the house and saw my bridge painting leaning against the living-room wall, I wanted to turn and run. Of course I couldn't because Mom was sitting right there on the stairs waiting for me. Sherlock left her side and came to me. I patted his head absently. I looked at the painting and cringed, then I dared to look at her. She had that expression on her face, the one that means I'm in for a long talk and she's expecting a lot of good explanations, not excuses. I knew the smartest thing to do was wait for her to start the conversation. So I stood there with my head down, like a dog that's been scolded.

"Your principal called. She said you ditched period three."

Kaboom! Mom likes to get right to the point.

"I'm sorry," I said. It's always good to start off with an apology, never a defence. "I didn't mean to miss class but I was working on a sculpture at lunch and lost track of time."

"You know your academic work is just as important as your art," she said.

"I know. I didn't mean to miss class."

"I was worried about you. I tried to call but you didn't pick up."

I pulled my phone out of my pocket and saw there were three missed calls.

"Oooops. I had the ringer turned off. Mrs. Galloway hates phones in her classroom."

Mom sighed out loud with defeat and I sighed inside with relief. If she hadn't been blocking the stairs, I would have fled to my room. But when she turned her attention to the painting, I braced myself.

"I don't think I need to tell you where I found this." The sarcasm in her voice was as thick as ketchup and she didn't wait for me to answer. "I thought you said you gave it to Mrs. Galloway?"

I wondered if I could get away with back-to-back apologies and decided it was my only chance.

"I'm sorry I lied. I just don't like the painting. I find it depressing." The last word caught in my throat.

"I'm beginning to worry about you, Anna."

I tried not to flinch. It was a bad sign when she said my name that way. It meant a lecture was coming. The dread made me feel dizzy.

"You've been distant lately, not your regular self. Now you're ditching classes and lying. Is there something going on at school?"

"It was one class and nothing's going on at school. I'm fine."

"You're not having problems with your friends? I know how mean teenage girls can be. I was in high school once too, you know."

"I'm fine," I repeated quickly, praying to any higher being who might be paying attention that she wouldn't launch into one of her high school stories.

"Boy trouble?"

"Mom! There's nothing going on. I'm fine. I just missed class because I have a sculpture due next week and it's taking longer than I expected."

She stood up finally and I felt a rush of relief. At least there was a clear path to my bedroom. But then she stepped over and wrapped her arms around me.

"Just promise you'll talk to me if you do have a problem."

"I promise," I said and waited for her to finish hugging me.

# ALIYA

Kyle moped around all summer and beat himself up about not asking Anna out for a cup of coffee the night of the art exhibit. He found me on Facebook at least once a week to ask how she was and what she was doing.

"Why don't you friend her so you can see for yourself what she's doing?" I wrote. It was a reasonable suggestion.

"I am her friend, but she's never online anymore."

"OMG!" I wrote back that blistering August day when I was feeling impatient from the heat. "Stop torturing us both and call her then. Ask her to a movie or something."

"I don't know what she'd like to see."

For once I was actually relieved we lived on opposite sides of the city. He was like a curly headed Eeyore — down about everything.

"Then *ask* her what *she'd* like to see."

"It'd seem too weird. Maybe it'd be better if we went out all together. Something more random."

"You want me to be the third wheel and chaperone your date? No thanks!"

"Some friend you are. Won't even help a guy out. ☺"

"Some friend YOU are, torturing a nice girl like me!" I logged off without saying goodbye. I didn't feel bad either. I figured it would serve him right to suffer alone for the night.

Kyle's perfect random event finally happened near the end of September in grade eleven. His older brother, Sam, and a bunch of grade-twelve guys organized a party down at the forks, which is just below the West River Viaduct where the river splits in two. Organizing a party at the forks isn't really all that difficult. You just have to put out the word about when you're having a party and show up. The hardest part is being popular enough to interest a crowd. Sometimes three hundred kids will show up and make such a commotion the cops have to come and bust things up. That happened to Anna's brother when we were in grade nine. He got charged with drinking under age. Anna's parents were furious. I remember being over for dinner later that week and nobody spoke a word at the table. It was the most uncomfortable meal of my life. At least Mom and I watch TV so we don't have to listen to ourselves chew.

Anyhow, even by grade eleven I'd never been to a party at the forks or to any party where drinking was involved. My mom was not big on teenage drinking or partying or generally letting me have any fun. So when Kyle invited me and hinted that I should bring Anna, I laughed out loud in his face.

"Do you listen to anything I say?" I asked. "Do you remember I have the most overprotective mother in the en-*tire* world? She makes the Queen of England seem laid back."

We were walking down the hall toward my locker at the end of the day.

"Maybe you could sleep at Anna's overnight. Then your mom wouldn't know."

"So you're asking me to lie to my mother?"

"Not really. You'd still be sleeping at Anna's."

"I dunno. When I sleep over at a friend's place, she asks about everything we'll be doing. And she can smell a lie ten miles away."

"Just try it. Say you're working on some art assignment together."

"Let me think about it," I said. Then I opened my locker and piled my books on the top shelf.

That night I thought of nothing else but the party at the forks. I hated to admit it, but I really wanted to go and Kyle's plan sounded like it might work. Finally I logged on to Facebook and saw Anna was online for a change.

"There's a big party down at the forks this weekend," I wrote.

"Really? You going?"

"Mom wouldn't let me go in a hundred years. What about your parents?"

"Not likely since Joe's adventure down there. But Mariam's parents are going away this weekend. Maybe we could have a sleepover. Then nobody would know!"

"Good plan. But I'd have to say I was staying at your place. Mom doesn't know Mariam's parents. She'd want to talk to them. It could get complicated."

"Tell your mom you're sleeping over here and I'll tell my parents I'm sleeping at Mariam's. Then we can all go to the party and crash at Mariam's. It's closest to the forks anyway."

"Awesome plan! Check with Mariam and let me know."

About ten minutes later, Anna's chat box opened up again.

"Wooohooo! It's all set. Mariam's in," she wrote.

I could hardly wait to tell Kyle the good news in person. We were sitting in the cafeteria at lunch when I finally saw him. Anna, Mariam, Gisele, and I were talking about our sleepover when he walked up.

"So are you guys coming to the forks Saturday night?" he asked. He set down his lunch and pulled up a chair.

Mariam and Gisele made a hooting sound that meant "yes." Anna looked unsure and I was afraid to say too much in case my mother figured out what we were up to and wrecked my plans at the last minute.

"So that sleepover idea worked?"

"Yep. My parents actually thought it was a good idea for me to have some girlfriends over so I wouldn't be alone," Mariam said.

Kyle told us he'd be at the forks by nine o'clock. He also couldn't help but mention this would be the third party he'd been to there. I'm sure he was trying to be helpful but it was kind of annoying.

"Don't wear any girly shoes. Boots or running shoes work best down there once it gets dark. And no skirts. Definitely jeans and sweaters."

I rolled my eyes and Anna said, "It sounds like we're going camping. Should I bring my Swiss Army knife?"

Anna can be pretty sarcastic when she wants to be.

Kyle smiled. "If you have one."

"What about beer?" Mariam asked. She's always one to be practical. If we were going to a party we needed something to drink.

"Sam can hook us up. No worries. They're going to have a bin with ice and a keg."

"How're they going to get a keg down to the forks?" I asked, skeptically.

"They have their ways."

To my surprise, it was easy letting Mom think I was sleeping over at Anna's, probably because I did that fairly regularly. Anna's parents barely blinked when we left together for Mariam's sleepover and Mariam's parents even left us a houseful of teenager-friendly food like pizza pockets and chocolate cake. It was almost dark when the four of us decided to leave Mariam's house. We were at the door spraying ourselves with bug repellent when Mariam said, "Okay, girls, does everyone have their cellphone?"

We patted our pockets and nodded.

"Cash in case of emergencies?"

Again we nodded collectively.

"Flashlights?"

We aimed our flashlights at Mariam and turned them on. She shielded her face and laughed.

"I've got the house keys so were all set. Let's head out."

We talked and laughed as we walked toward the river. I could tell we were all excited. Even Anna seemed more talkative than she had in a long time. I figured it was a good sign, that maybe she was finally getting over her grandparents' death a little. Of course I knew I couldn't come out and ask her, even though I'd wanted to many times. Mariam took up a good ten minutes of the walk talking about how hot Sam was, then Gisele asked if Ray was going. I assured her Ray would be there because wherever Sam was, Ray was always close by.

When we got to the trail at the top of River Road, we started walking single file because although the path is paved, it's narrow and steep. It wasn't long before the glow from the streetlights got swallowed up by the trees, and we flicked on our flashlights.

"It's kind of creepy coming down here in the dark," I said.

"Don't worry. We're all together. We can protect each other," Mariam said.

"Easy for you to say, you're in the middle."

Anna was leading us through the forest when she stopped and turned off her flashlight. We piled up behind her.

"Stop for a minute," she said. "Turn off your flashlights."

We stood quietly in the darkness. I could hear cars in the distance rumbling over the viaduct and along River Road. I could hear a siren wailing in the distance and a car horn blaring. Down the hill we could hear voices and laughter and see the faint glow of a bonfire rising up above the treetops.

"That must be them. I can't believe they lit a fire," Gisele said. "Talk about a cop magnet."

"It'll be fine," Mariam said. "Let's go."

Mariam tried to move forward but Anna was blocking the path.

"Just hold on. Check out the stars," she said.

We looked up at the night sky through the gap in the trees. There were millions of tiny pricks in the darkness. I hadn't seen so many stars in my life.

"We're far enough away from the streetlights we can see them for a change," Anna said.

"You should see them at our cottage," Gisele said. "You can see Mars sometimes."

A gigantic whoop rose up from down the hillside. Anna sighed slightly and started walking again. As we got closer we could hear music and a chorus of voices. I felt like a warrior sneaking up on the enemy through the dark. The paved path gave way to a rough dirt path and although we weren't sure where we were going, we followed the noise through the forest. Finally we came to where we could see a slight clearing below. We could see the backs of at least fifty people and a bonfire blazing in the middle. When we got closer I saw Kyle, Sam, and Ray standing on the far side. Their faces were lit up and they were laughing. As soon as we walked into the circle of light, Sam whistled and hooted.

"All right! More hot girls!" he shouted. A wave of cheers rose up in response.

Beyond the fire there was a plastic tub full of ice and a keg of beer perched on top. A stack of red plastic cups was propped against a stump. A few kids were talking and waiting to fill up.

Kyle walked around the fire to where we were standing.

"Hey, you guys made it," he said.

"Hey, Kyle," we said in unison.

"It was a bit tricky getting down, but luckily Anna knows her way around the ravine," I added.

Kyle pulled over a log so we could sit down, then went to get some cups of beer. Mariam didn't stay long before she went to chat up Sam, and Gisele followed at her heels. I glanced over at Anna. She was staring intently at the fire and glowing in the firelight.

Kyle was back quickly. He sat down beside me and handed Anna and me each a beer. Mariam and Gisele were drinking theirs already.

"So no trouble from your mom?" Kyle asked me.

"It was pretty easy, actually."

We did a cheers with our plastic cups to celebrate our success in deceiving my mother.

"Wicked bonfire, don't you think?" Kyle leaned out past me and directed his question at Anna.

She took a sip of her beer and smiled. "I love watching fires."

Kids kept arriving until they were standing three people deep around the fire. Off in the darkness of the forest, I could hear people stumbling around, talking and laughing. One girl screamed that she'd just peed on her foot and everyone howled. Most of the other kids were from Ray and Sam's school, which was attached to Bachman by the cafeteria, so although I didn't know them by name, I recognized most of them. There were also a lot of performance kids, but nobody from the visual arts stream. I watched one of the grade-twelve guys from Sam's school head into the trees with one of the performance girls and a group of kids were dancing on the other side of the keg. One guy stumbled and tripped but two girls pulled him out of the way before he fell in the fire. When he was standing again they all hugged and laughed.

"This is so much fun," I said to Kyle and Anna, then took a long drink of my beer.

Kyle grabbed my glass and peered into Anna's. "You need a refill yet?"

Anna shook her head but I nodded and drained my cup, then handed it to Kyle. Anna watched him walk through the firelight to the keg.

"I think I have to pee soon!" I giggled. "Do you want to come?"

"I'm okay for a while," she said.

When I stood up I felt light-headed from the beer, but I stepped over the log anyway and headed toward the darkness.

"If I'm not back in five minutes come looking."

"Watch out for the river," Anna said.

Walking into the shadowy forest was disorienting and I stumbled over a branch. As soon as I got back up, I walked into a stump. I laughed to myself, then flicked on my flashlight to look around the pockets of darkness. I'd never peed in the forest in the middle of the night and it started to creep me out. I found a large tree and stepped into its shadow. I just wanted to get my business over and get back to the fire.

Neither Kyle nor Anna was anywhere in sight when I got back. At first I was annoyed and then I thought maybe Kyle would find the courage to talk to her alone and he'd stop bugging me all the time. I went over to Mariam and Gisele.

"Aliya!" Sam draped his arm over my shoulder. It felt like a gorilla was hanging over me. "Looks like you need another beer." He turned toward the keg and shouted: "Kyle, can you bring Aliya another one of those beers?"

Kyle emerged from the shadows and handed me another red cup. I took a drink and looked around.

"Where'd Anna go?" I asked him.

"I thought she went with you?"

My heart tripped. "Mariam? Have you seen Anna?"

Mariam shook her head and swayed to the music. "She probably just had to pee or something."

I suddenly remembered the last time I'd been at the forks. I'd been with Anna and her Granny. We'd spent a warm fall day tucked up between the rocks and trees, sketching detailed close-ups of leaves and flowers, bugs and butterflies. Anna had spent two hours at the very edge of the river drawing a series of the water lapping at the rocks. There was only one place that you could get right to the water, without having to scramble down the steep riverbank.

I tugged on Kyle's shirt until he was leaning by my face. "We better go find her," I said.

Kyle grabbed a fresh beer out of Sam's hand.

"Let's do it," he said.

I pulled out my flashlight and headed toward the river while Kyle followed.

"Do you have any idea where you're going?" he called out.

"I've been down here a few times."

It was slow going and even though I had the flashlight, I slammed my shin into a log hidden in the undergrowth.

"Stupid log," I muttered and rubbed my leg.

Although there were plenty of stars above, the moon was just a sliver in the sky and the reach of the fire was too limited to offer any comfort. The air was also a lot cooler and damper the farther away we got.

"Crap," Kyle said. "I just spilled a whole cup of beer down my shirt."

I turned and shone my flashlight on him. Sure enough, his shirt was drenched.

"Don't worry, it'll dry out when you get back to the fire. C'mon. I bet she's up here."

We got turned around more than once, but when we finally got to the river Anna wasn't there. I shined the flashlight up and down the banks.

"Anna?" I called out. "Anna? Are you down here?"

I heard a splashing and I spun around. My heart raced. "Anna?"

But I didn't find her. I found Kyle instead, bent over the river, rinsing his shirt in the water.

"What are you doing?"

"Washing the beer out of my shirt. If Mom smells it she'll know I was drinking."

"Good thing you didn't spill beer on your pants."

"Yeah, good thing," Kyle said in a monotone. "She'll kill me if she finds out."

"Oh, for God sakes, I'm sure she knows you drink by now." I squatted on the riverbank beside him.

"She thinks Sam is the bad one and I'm the innocent one." He shivered. "It's freaking cold out here."

"It is when you're half naked." I laughed. Then I put my hand on his back to see how cold he felt.

He squealed and jumped away. "Your hands are freezing."

"You feel warm to me," I said. "Now hurry up."

That's when I heard branches snapping in the bushes and I froze.

"Anna?" I called out. I turned and followed the crashing sound through the darkness. Kyle trailed after, ringing out his shirt as he went.

"Hey, watch where you're walking," some guy said in the darkness. A girl giggled and I flashed my light sideways to see I'd almost tripped over a couple lying in a patch of tall grass.

When we got back to the fire I still couldn't find Anna and by that time there were twice as many kids and ten times the noise. Drunk teenagers get exponentially louder by the hour. I pushed my way through the crowd to Mariam and Gisele.

"Where've you been?" Mariam shouted. Then she flopped an arm over my shoulder and kissed my cheek. "We missed you."

"Hey, why is Kyle half undressed?" Sam bellowed.

Of course everyone turned to stare and it looked like we'd just stumbled out of the darkness together. I ignored the taunts and turned to Gisele, hoping she was a bit more sober.

"Have you seen Anna?"

"Not for a while. Where've you and Kyle been, anyway?"

"Looking for her," I said. "C'mon and help us."

I pulled Gisele away from the fire and together we searched the forest. I even tried calling her cellphone, but she didn't pick up. I thought about calling her house to see if she'd gone home, but it was late and I couldn't very well wake up her mother and tell her I'd lost Anna in the ravine.

I went back to where Kyle was drying his shirt by the fire.

"Did you find her?" he asked.

"No. I'm going to get the girls and go back to Mariam's. Maybe she went there."

"Text me when you find her."

I could tell he wasn't having fun anymore. With Anna missing, the party didn't seem like fun to me either. Kids were sprawled all over the place and during one of my searches, I heard someone throwing up behind a tree. Finally I dragged Mariam away from the fire and told her it was time to go home.

"But I'm having fun!" she said.

"I heard the cops are on their way and we should get out of here before we get caught."

It was a lie, but it sobered her up pretty fast.

I headed up the path as fast as I could while Mariam stumbled behind me and Gisele supported her as much as she could. When we got to River Road, Mariam pulled out her cellphone.

"Oh, look. I have a text! It's from Farah. She says: Anna felt like crap so I gave her a ride home. She says not to worry. See you Monday."

I hadn't even seen Farah at the party, but there were probably a hundred kids I never saw.

The next morning when I woke up I had a sick feeling in my stomach, and not just from the beer. I was afraid Anna had seen Kyle and me by the river. When I got home I logged on to Facebook, but Anna wasn't online. I sent her an email but she didn't write back. I tried to call her cellphone five times and left two messages, but either her battery was dead or she was ignoring me. As a last resort I called her house, but the answering machine picked up. Finally, a chat box popped up on my laptop. It was Kyle.

"Did you talk to Anna?"

"Can't find her."

"But she's okay?"

"Think so."

"Do you think she saw us by the river?"

"Hope not."

"Me too ☹," he wrote back.

I didn't see Anna until Monday morning in class. She already had her brushes and paints out and was working on a watercolour of the city skyline.

"You scared us Saturday night. Kyle and I looked all over for you." I didn't mean to sound like I was scolding her but I couldn't help myself.

"Sorry," she said without looking at me. "I didn't mean to scare you. But I wasn't feeling well and Farah was heading home so I thought I'd catch a ride."

"You should have at least told me you were leaving." I sounded like my mother and cringed.

"I couldn't find you," she said flatly. "Or Kyle."

I paused but I wasn't ready to start defending myself. If she hadn't seen us, I knew it would just make me look guilty.

"You could have told Mariam or Gisele, anybody."

"I told Tyson to tell you. Didn't he give you my message?"

"Uh, no. It must have slipped his mind," I said. I couldn't even recall seeing Tyson Saturday night.

I stood there for a few more minutes while Anna continued to paint. I couldn't tell if she was lying or not. It wasn't until I found Farah later in the day that I realized she was definitely lying, or at least not telling the whole truth.

"Farah!" I called out from down the hall. Farah was just closing her locker and heading toward the music room.

"I heard you were at the forks Saturday night. I didn't see you," I said, breathlessly, when I caught up to her.

"I never made it, actually. I ran into Anna on the way down the hill and she begged me to take her home. She was soaked and crying. Didn't she tell you? She said she went for a pee and fell in the river."

I went along with the story and didn't press Farah for more information. But inside my head, alarms were blaring. I'd never known Anna to cry and, even in the dark, I was sure she knew the area too well to accidentally fall in the river.

# ANNA'S MOM

After my husband made the connection between my parents' accident and Anna's painting of the viaduct, I started to watch her more carefully, without letting on how concerned I was. But what was there to see, really, besides a regular, moody teenage girl? I never quite knew when she was going to throw back a joke if I teased or when she was going to give me that withering look of contempt and storm off to her room. But I remembered being the same when I was sixteen, so I did my best not to overreact. I didn't want her to have an excuse to build barriers between us. Without my mother to mediate, I knew I needed to save whatever connection we had.

I didn't say another word about her painting, but I wrapped it back up in plastic and stored it in the attic where it wouldn't get damp. I thought maybe someday we could get it framed and hang it in the dining room, but for the time being she didn't need it staring at her during family dinners. She never once asked what happened to it and I think, with everything else going on, we forgot about that lonely girl standing in the middle of a misty bridge.

That fall though, life with Anna became unpredictable. It was more than just being moody. For the first time she started to act out of character. It wasn't simply that she missed a class or lied about the painting. Late one night she came home soaked from head to toe. It wasn't only strange because she arrived home wet in the middle of the night, it was also strange because she wasn't supposed to be coming home at all. She had plans to sleep over at a girlfriend's house.

My husband was away on business and I was alone, so I had Sherlock in the bedroom with me. It was close to midnight when I heard him push open the bedroom door and run downstairs. When he didn't bark, I knew it was Anna or Joe and that, in either case, something was wrong. I turned on the bedroom light, wrapped a robe around myself, and headed quickly down the hall. The front entrance was in complete darkness so I flipped on the light switch. Anna was in the front entrance, bent over taking off one of her running shoes while Sherlock licked her ear.

"Sweetheart! Are you okay?" I asked.

She looked up quickly and I could tell I'd startled her.

"I'm fine," she muttered. Then she tackled the other shoe.

It took me a second to realize why she was struggling so much. The shoes were wet, her jeans were wet, her jean jacket was wet. I could tell her hair had been wet too. And she was shivering from the cold. I rushed over to help her out of her wet jacket but she pulled away.

"I'll get it," she said.

"What happened to you?"

"I'm fine," she repeated.

I could smell beer on her and I felt my pulse race. I wasn't sure if I should be worried or angry and since both emotions were swelling inside me, I didn't have a chance of staying calm.

"Anna!" I said too sharply. "You're soaked and you smell like beer. It's almost midnight. I deserve to know what's going on."

"I fell in the water."

That's when I noticed her lips were blue and she was having a hard time talking.

"I'll start the shower. You need to get warmed up."

She finished peeling off her wet clothes while I went to the bathroom and started the shower. I got a clean towel and put it on the vanity, then checked the temperature of the water. As I left the bathroom, Anna brushed past me in her wet underwear. I could see goosebumps on her arms.

"Get yourself good and warm, then we can talk," I said. Then I left the bathroom and closed the door.

Even though I was desperate to know what happened, I told myself the most important thing was that she was safe. I made myself breathe deeply and count to ten so I wouldn't go back into the bathroom and try to talk through the shower curtain. I knew if I pressed her it would only make things worse. Instead, I went and picked up her wet clothes from the floor by the front door. Her shoes were muddy and there were bits of dead leaves stuck to them. I bundled the entire mess in my arms and dumped it in the laundry room. Then I went back to my bedroom to wait.

Anna was in the shower for twenty minutes but I didn't once knock on the door to see how she was doing. It took a lot of restraint. I thought about calling my husband or Joe, but until I found out what had happened I didn't think I should worry either of them. Finally Anna emerged from the bathroom and scuttled into her room. I heard her moving about and then everything was quiet. When I couldn't stand waiting another minute, I knocked on her bedroom door.

"Anna?" I said quietly. She didn't answer so I knocked again and walked in. She was tucked deep under her covers with her back to me.

"Anna, I need to know what happened tonight."

"Can we talk in the morning? I'm beat." She didn't roll over to face me.

"I won't sleep if I don't find out what happened. Why are you coming home so late soaking wet and smelling of beer? I thought you were sleeping over at Mariam's?"

"I changed my mind," she said.

It was obvious she didn't want to talk about what happened, but I couldn't let it go.

"I want to know why you changed your mind and I suspect it has something to do with you coming home wet, so stop avoiding my questions and just tell me."

"I'm not avoiding anything." She sighed deeply, as if I was being a huge pain in the butt and she wanted me to know. "The girls started drinking beer and getting rowdy, and I just didn't feel comfortable, so I came home."

Her explanation was so mature it winded me, and for a moment I sat on the edge of her bed trying to sort out my thoughts.

"Were you drinking?"

"No, but someone spilled some on me. Can I go to sleep now?"

"How did you get home?"

"I took a cab."

"Why didn't you call me? You know I'd have come over no matter what time it was."

"I didn't want you to know they were drinking." She rolled over on her back and stared up at me. She looked embarrassed and I suddenly felt bad for making her tell on her friends.

"I'm glad you came home, but I really wish you'd called for a ride."

"I was okay."

"Still," I said. "Parents want to do those sorts of things for their kids."

"I'm sorry. I'll remember for next time."

"How did you get wet, anyway?"

"The girls threw me in Mariam's pool."

"I didn't know Mariam's family had a pool. You poor thing. You must have been freezing. Why didn't you change before you left?"

"I only had my pajamas with me and I just wanted to get home."

"Was Aliya drinking?"

She paused. "No, it wasn't us. Some other girls showed up. Some girls from BHS that Mariam knows. She wanted them to leave but they wouldn't."

"Were there boys?"

"No, just these girls. About seven or eight of them."

"Are they still over there? Should I go over and see if everything is okay?"

"No, no." Anna said quickly. "I think it's probably under control now. Can I please go to sleep? I'm so tired."

"Of course," I said and stood up. I tucked the comforter tight around her the way I did when she was a little girl and kissed her on the cheek. "Sleep tight."

I made sure the front door was locked then went back to bed. It took me a long time to fall asleep, and as I did the questions

I should have asked scrolled through my mind. Why didn't she borrow some clothes from Mariam before she came home? Why were her shoes covered in mud and leaves? If she got thrown in a pool, why didn't her clothes smell like chlorine? Where did those girls get the beer? Would she have minded if I'd lain with her awhile, just until she fell asleep, the way I did when she was little?

There was one long ago night that stood out in my memory suddenly, a bedtime that ended in tears when Anna was about four years old. She had always been mature for her age, even as a very young girl, and yet it still threw me off guard twelve years later. You'd think I'd get used to it.

"Stay with me," she begged when the bedtime story was over and I leaned past her to turn out the light. I often lay with her until she fell asleep. If I didn't, she complained that lying flat in the darkness felt like being dead.

"I'll stay, but just until you to go to sleep," I said.

"Okay," she agreed and moved close to the wall to make room for me.

I lay down beside her and fought to stay awake after a long day of work.

"Are you asleep?" she asked after a few minutes.

"No."

"Okay, good. Don't leave yet. I'm still awake," she said in her sleepy little voice. Then she yawned.

"I won't leave until you go to sleep," I promised. It was one I'd made a hundred times.

"When I die will you still love me?" she asked suddenly.

The question startled me but I tried to stay calm so sleep would come to her faster.

"I'll love you no matter what, sweetheart. But you're going to live much longer than me."

"How do you know?"

"Because I'm older than you. When I'm old like Granny, you'll still be young and healthy."

"Is Granny going to die soon?" She sounded alarmed.

"No, Granny still has a lot of life left in her."

"How much?"

"Years and years. Now stop talking and go to sleep." I couldn't help but think of the dinner dishes that needed washing and the laundry waiting to be folded.

"When are you going to die?" she asked. Her breath caught in her throat and I knew she was going to cry so I pulled her close and kissed the top of her head.

"I don't know when, but not for a long time yet. I promise."

"What if I still need you?" she sobbed.

"By the time I die, you won't need me anymore."

Her little body shuddered and then she sighed. "I hope you won't need me anymore by the time I die too," she said.

The day after the failed sleepover, she slept until noon. Part of me thought she was hiding in her room so she wouldn't have to face me, but I didn't hear any sounds either, even when I stopped and listened at her door. By the time I heard the shower running, I'd washed and dried her wet clothes and set her shoes out in the sun. I'd also talked to Joe.

"I'm sure you'll make it worse if you go in there and wake her up. She probably had a fight with Aliya and feels stupid. Just let her get up on her own," he said over the phone.

"Don't you think it's crazy though? Coming home in the middle of the night wet like that?"

"No crazier than some of the stuff I did back then. I mean, come on. This is Anna we're talking about. It's actually pretty responsible of her to bail on a party because she was feeling weird about what was going on."

"I guess, but you should have seen her. She looked like she'd been crying and she was blue from shivering."

"She'd probably been wet for forty minutes by then," Joe said. "And if she had a fight with the girls, she might have stormed off. Don't make too much out of it."

"Okay, you're right," I agreed. But still, I didn't feel good about letting it drop either.

"And, Mom?"

"Yes, honey?"

"Maybe you better not tell Dad. He'll just get all worked up. And besides, you'll score more points for next time if you keep her secret."

"Is that how you operate?" I asked.

"Something like that." He laughed.

When Anna finally appeared, she acted as if nothing unusual had happened and I let the whole thing drop. But when the phone rang she tensed up.

"It's probably Aliya," she muttered. "Let the machine get it. I'll call her later."

I nodded and offered to make her some scrambled eggs and toast. For a change she agreed and it felt good to be needed again, as if some of the balance was restored. I put the plate of eggs in front of her and made myself leave the kitchen so I wouldn't sit and watch her eat. It seemed as if Joe was right and she was going through the regular ups and downs of being a teenage girl.

"You want to go to a movie tonight?" she asked later in the day.

The suggestion surprised me, but I was happy she wanted to be with me at all. It seemed like a good way to spend some time with her, even if there wouldn't be much chance to talk.

# ANNA

I'm still not sure what happened the night of the party. One minute I was sitting on a log drinking beer out of a red plastic cup and the next I was slipping through the forest, hoping nobody noticed me leave. When I got to the edge of the river, I sat down and watched the water ripple in the stray rays of moonlight. I was at the part of the river where the bank is steep and the river deep, on a bend where years of erosion have made it impossible to get down to the water's edge. I'd been there many times before with Granny. It was one of our favourite sketching spots.

I watched the river and listened to the party going on behind me in the distance, as if it was the party of another girl in another time, a girl who belonged among the laughter and dancing. Even though I knew I'd come willingly to the party, it was hard to connect myself to it. I felt disoriented, like the thread that kept me attached to the time and place of being Anna was stretched too thin and I was about to disappear completely or slip into another reality. The images in front of my eyes started to blur and I was fighting to hold on to consciousness. In that moment I wasn't aware of thinking or breathing or of even being alive. I don't know how long the confusion took over, but suddenly I found myself tumbling down the steep riverbank. I plunged into the river headfirst, then quickly came up fighting for air and choking on water. I couldn't touch the bottom and the weight of my clothes started to drag me down, but I was much too good of a swimmer to let myself sink under the surface again.

*Did I jump or fall?* I wondered as I frantically clawed my way to shore. I couldn't get a good hold on the steep riverbank so I had to flow with the current until I found the one shallow place where the bank meets the water in a gradual slope. I pulled myself onto land, then into some nearby bushes to catch my breath and collect my thoughts.

I considered calling someone for help but I was shivering so hard I could barely dial my cellphone. I quickly realized it didn't matter though, because the phone was so waterlogged it was probably never going to dry out. *Who would I call anyway?* I wondered through my chattering teeth. I couldn't very well call Mom to tromp through the bush until she found me, and I didn't want to face Aliya or the others. Dad was in Chicago and the only other person I could think of was Joe. I knew Joe could keep a secret, but I didn't want to have to explain to him what had happened. He might remember the day I wandered across the bridge, and get suspicious.

I felt my jacket pocket and realized I'd also lost my flashlight. That's when I really started to panic. My pulse was racing and my mind was flying about a million miles an hour. I needed to get home, but I wasn't sure how. I wasn't even sure how long I'd been away from the party. It seemed like hours but time was hard to track in the darkness and it might have only been a few minutes. I still had the emergency cash tucked into the pocket of my jeans, so at the very least I knew I could catch a cab home if I could get up to River Road. It would be tough going in wet clothes in the dark, but I was familiar with the area so it was worth a shot. Besides, I couldn't think of anything else to do. Avoiding drunk teenagers, especially Aliya, was going to be the real challenge.

I took a deep breath and stood up. I felt unsteady on my feet from shaking, but I hoped that once I started moving, I'd warm up. Then I heard voices coming toward me and instinctively I crouched down again. I heard Aliya call my name and saw the beam of her flashlight slice through the trees. At one point the light brushed past my cheek and I laid myself flat on the ground. My initial urge was to go to her, go back to the fire and get warm, but I knew I couldn't let her see me dripping wet. She'd turn it into a huge drama. I revaluated my options and again decided my best bet was to get home and sneak into bed without waking Mom.

Of course, my idea didn't go off exactly as planned, but thanks to some quick thinking and good timing, I found a ride home. I also managed to keep Mom from completely freaking out when she found me sneaking into the house wet. It turns out the only witnesses to the whole ordeal were Farah and Mom and both seemed to buy into my story. Still, I thought it was best to play it low key for a few days, or even a couple of weeks, until there was a new party for everyone to get distracted by.

I figured the biggest problem was going to be lying to Aliya, and I was right. The Monday after the party she let me know she wasn't very happy I'd left without telling her.

I acted like it was no big deal so she'd drop the whole thing, which worked for the most part. But she carried a grudge for a few weeks. She didn't email or call and she didn't come over to my house either. She also started spending more time at school with Kyle, which was pretty much inevitable anyway. Even though Aliya insists they're just friends and have been since junior high, I know they have a thing for each other.

Despite the fact I'd managed to pull off, like, the biggest lie in the world, the whole thing freaked me out — not only because I'd ended up in the river, but because I'd done it without realizing what I was doing. It was like some external force took over my body and threw me into the water. The other thing that bothered me was how strongly my body fought back. I realized I was up against more than just being afraid of heights and blood. I was up against a survival instinct, and no matter how badly I might want to escape, my body wanted to keep walking around this world. I knew that if I ever tried to kill myself for real, I'd need a foolproof plan. I'd have to choose something where there was no turning back — like jumping off a bridge. Once I jumped, theoretically speaking, my body couldn't fight its way to safety. Of course, I knew the challenge was going to be tricking my body into thinking it was safe until the very last second. And although I had no idea what might work, I was open to suggestions, especially since my options were starting to dwindle.

That Halloween a solution presented itself. Although I'd always found hangings creepy, the night of Halloween a boy did hang himself, from a tree on the boulevard in front of Thomas Jackson Secondary School. He was dressed in a vampire costume and the kids who arrived early thought it was a Halloween joke, like a prop from the drama room. Then someone dared someone else to go touch it. Apparently that's when the girls started screaming and the school went berserk. Everyone in the whole city was talking about it and it was all over the news.

"I mean, it was so random," Aliya said at lunch a few days later. Our routine had almost returned to normal by then, and we were sitting together in the cafeteria.

"I heard his parents didn't have a clue anything was wrong," Gisele added.

*Why would they?* I thought. *It's so easy to live a lie.* But instead of saying anything I bit into my hamburger. It was like chewing an old dog toy.

"My cousin goes to Thomas Jackson. He said this guy was picked on every day at school. Bullied right from grade one. Then someone started a Facebook group called Make Justin's Life Hell. There were four hundred members. People would tell him right to his face that he'd be better off dead. I guess he cracked finally," Mariam said.

"I know someone who goes there too. Apparently his best friend is so freaked out they've sedated him. Can you imagine how you'd feel if your best friend killed themselves?" Aliya said.

I shivered. *Did she look at me when she said that?*

"I guess it just goes to show you don't know people as well as you think," I said in a neutral tone.

"It's true," Aliya said, and this time she looked at me directly. "People you think you know inside and out can have some pretty scary secrets. Like my mom. I didn't find out until two years ago she had a sister who killed herself in high school. My whole life I never heard anyone even mention her name. Mom never talks about her. My grandparents never talk about her. There's not a single picture of her anywhere. It's like she's been erased. I only found out by accident because I was snooping through one of Mom's old high school yearbooks and saw they had the same last name."

The confession shocked me, but I didn't let on. I wondered, though, why Aliya was sharing it suddenly, after more than two years. I started to worry that she was catching on to my plan.

That afternoon during math, when the teacher was reviewing the results of a recent test, I thought about Justin, the boy who hanged himself. I stared at the teacher like I might be listening, but what I was really thinking about was how my death might affect people. I knew the immediate shock would be horrible for Mom and Dad, and even Joe. Mom would have the police at her door again and there would be stories all over the news to remind them for weeks, maybe months. Aliya might even lose it herself, especially since her mother was already overprotective and would start to hold on tighter. I thought about how Mariam would take it, and Gisele, and my teachers. I thought about Mrs. Galloway telling me I had so much potential as an artist and how she would say to her husband after that it was a waste of talent. I knew the school would be turned upside down with grief and gossip for a few days. I knew lots of people would be upset. I just didn't think it was a good enough reason to keep me tied to them. I thought they'd be better off without me moping around all the time. I mean, Mom was slowly getting over Granny and Gramps. She'd probably get over me too. I thought of all this while the teacher droned on and on. When the day finally ended, it was a huge relief to go home.

Aliya and I sometimes end up on the same bus home. She lives in the same direction but catches a second bus just past my stop. That day I got to the bus stop early and waited alone. When it arrived, I flashed my student card at the driver and took a seat near the back. Aliya ran on just before the doors closed. She dropped into the seat beside me and put her book bag on her knees.

"You're a brainiac. Did you get any of that stuff in math class?" She was breathing hard from sprinting up the street. I was annoyed she'd made it and I was going to have to talk the whole way home. I was afraid she'd want to continue the conversation about the guy from TJSS or, worse, her aunt.

I shook my head. "Nope. It went right over my head too."

"Crap," she said and slumped. "I thought for sure you'd know what was going on."

"I was reading something for language arts."

"Do you want to come over tonight and we can try and figure it out together?"

I was surprised by the invitation. I hadn't been to her house or had her over to my house since before the party at the forks.

"Okay, I'll see if Mom can drop me by after dinner."

The bus pulled to my stop and I waved back to Aliya before I jumped off. I crossed the street and cut through the park. There was a mother with two children playing on the swings. She was giving them underdogs and pretending to catch their feet. I stood and stared because suddenly I realized the swing set would be the perfect place. I sat down on a nearby bench to think it through. I didn't know much about tying ropes, but I figured I could manage a few simple knots.

*It might be the perfect way to fool myself,* I thought. I'd been on swings since I was a child so my body wouldn't know to be afraid until it was too late.

A few minutes later the mother rounded up her kids and left the park. I was probably creeping her out. I wondered what she'd think if she found out a girl committed suicide on the very same swing set. But then I pushed it from my mind. I had enough to worry about without taking complete strangers into consideration.

Even before I went inside to let Sherlock out for a pee, I opened the garage door. Dad's a borderline hoarder so I was sure he'd have something. I snooped through crates and boxes until I found what I was looking for: a practice rope. On the way to Aliya's, I thought I could try making a noose, just as an experiment. Then I'd be ready when I needed an escape hatch.

After dinner was finished and the dishes done, I told Mom I was going over to Aliya's.

"Neither of us understood a thing in math today. We thought we might try and figure it out together."

"That's fine sweetie. Do you want a ride?"

"I'm okay taking the bus, and her mom's going to drop me back."

I went to my room and got my backpack. I emptied it except for my math books and slung it over my shoulder. I left my cellphone on my bed. I didn't want any distractions.

Before I headed to the park I stopped at the garage. I tucked the rope into my backpack, then closed the garage door as quietly as I could so Sherlock wouldn't start barking. Luckily for me, it was drizzling. That meant even the dog walkers wouldn't venture too far into the park. I'd have enough time to try making a noose and still catch the bus before Aliya started to worry.

I walked past the park to be sure it was empty, then circled back and hid in the shadows while I rigged the knots. It took a couple of throws before I got the rope over the top bar of the swing set, but as soon as I did, I pulled it tight. When I finished I stepped back to assess my effort. The loop was hanging at least seven feet off the ground. That meant, even if I stretched, my toes wouldn't be able to touch. I pulled hard on the rope and the knots held. I picked up my feet and let myself swing back and forth and, again, the knots held. I felt an odd mix of pride and hope because for the first time it seemed like I had a solid plan.

As a test, I stepped up onto one of the swings and steadied myself, then hooked the noose with my free arm. *It can't hurt just to go through the motions*, I thought, as I flipped it quickly over my head. My hands started to shake and my heart was racing so I knew my body was getting ready to rebel. *I'll take it off in a second*, I thought to myself. But I willed myself to stand silently for a moment so I'd get used to the feeling of having the rope around my neck.

I was reaching above my head to pull the rope off when I lost my balance. The swing shifted backward and my feet tilted forward. My heart started pounding. I fought to steady myself, but instead my body pitched forward until my feet were no longer standing on anything. Part of me couldn't believe what I'd done. I felt a surge of hope.

The hopeful disbelief soon gave way to panic though when the rope squeezed my throat. I couldn't get enough oxygen into my lungs, yet my brain was still processing thoughts. I saw images of the police finding my body, then knocking on the door and handing Mom and Dad my math books. I wondered if I'd regret dying.

The place where the rope circled my neck burned like fire and licks of pain ripped down my spine, but somehow I was still wheezing enough oxygen into my lungs to stay alive. My eyes teared up and I gasped over and over. Then I heard voices in the darkness and the adrenalin kicked in. More than anything I didn't want to be caught. I saw myself locked in a mental ward wearing a hospital gown and fear took over. I reached above my head and pulled up with all my strength. I kicked wildly at the same time. That's when I bumped the swing with my leg. I twisted my body and stepped back up on it. I clawed the noose loose and sucked back a huge lungful of air. Then I pulled the rope completely off my neck and fell to the dirt below.

I panted and wiped the tears off my cheeks. I wasn't crying exactly. It was a physical reaction more than an emotional one. Or maybe it was the frustration leaking out of me. I held my breath and glanced around. Two people were walking across the far side of the park. From the silhouette of their clothes I could tell they were wearing baggy jeans and ball caps. When they got closer my heart sputtered. It was Ray and Sam.

*What the hell are they doing in my neighbourhood, walking in the rain?* I wondered bitterly.

I grabbed my backpack and scurried into the shadows of the nearby trees. I thought I was going to throw up, but I took a steadying breath and controlled the urge.

"Hey, is that a noose?" I heard Ray say.

I hoped it wasn't still swinging or they'd know I was close by.

"Check it out," Sam said.

The park went silent and I knew they were looking around.

I breathed as quietly as I could and pinned my back to the tree trunk. I felt as trapped as a dead beetle in a glass case.

*Please don't let them find me here,* I prayed.

"It's probably a prank because of that guy at TJSS," Ray said.

"Yeah, who'd be stupid enough to off themselves here?"

"I don't even think this rope would be strong enough to hang someone. Look how stretchy it is!"

Their comments stung like lemon juice on a paper cut. If only I'd rolled myself off the bridge when I had the chance. Then I wouldn't be tormenting myself like this. Then I would already be free.

"You got your phone? Maybe we should call the police."

I think it was Sam talking. He was nothing like Kyle. He was the kind of guy who whistled at girls from across the street, the kind of guy who'd spill beer on you at a party and laugh instead of apologize. Kyle, he was different. He was the kind of guy you'd want to take home to your parents, if you were lucky enough.

"What time is it?" Sam asked. "We better keep track of the time."

"Five after eight," Ray said.

I rubbed my neck, then wiped the dirt off my jeans. It had been less than twenty minutes since I left the house and I knew I needed to get out of there fast, before the police showed up. While the boys looked up the number, I slung my backpack over my shoulder and sprinted through the trees as fast as my aching neck would let me. I got all the way home before I remembered I was supposed to be on my way to Aliya's.

"Anna? Is that you?" Mom came to the front door. Sherlock followed and licked the raindrops off my shoes.

I ducked down into my hoodie. "Yeah, it's me," I said. "It started raining."

"Your sweater's all wet. You better go change. Oh, and Aliya just called. She said you weren't answering your phone and wanted to make sure you'd left. What happened?"

"I got halfway there and realized I forgot my math books *and* my phone." I kicked off my shoes. "I'll go call her."

It took a lot of control not to run to my bedroom. I closed the door gently, then slumped to the floor and dropped my head on my knees. I'd almost done exactly what I didn't want to do. I was afraid to wonder how much further it was to the bottom.

Aliya called back before I'd collected myself enough to call her. Mom knocked on my bedroom door.

"Sweetie, it's for you. Aliya again."

"Got it, thanks!" I called out in what was meant to be my most carefree teenaged-girl voice. "Hey, Aliya. Sorry. I forgot my phone and my math books and by the time I caught a bus home, it was close to eight-thirty. Mom didn't want me going back out."

"You could have used my books," Aliya said irritably. I almost didn't blame her for sounding so pissed.

"Sorry, I didn't think it would take so long and I did some problems after school I thought might help us."

"Whatever. I thought your mom was going to drive you over?" Aliya said.

I took a deep breath. I was getting sloppy with my lies.

"She got home late. I'm sorry. I made a mess of your night. You want to meet in the morning?"

"I guess. Library at eight?"

"See you then," I said.

"Don't forget your math books this time."

"I won't." I managed to laugh, but it burned my throat.

It hadn't even been an hour and I could tell the noose was going to leave a nasty bruise around my neck. There was already a red ring under my chin and it hurt to swallow. I climbed into my pajamas and pulled my bathrobe high around my neck. Then I went to the washroom to take something for the headache that was starting to pound inside my skull.

If I thought I felt hollow before I'd almost hanged myself I was being a bigger suck than Sherlock during a thunderstorm, because when I lay down on my bed it felt like my entire being had dropped out of me. I used to think I didn't belong and that was why being alive felt so uncomfortable, but it was way beyond that. I might have been able to live with the loneliness of not belonging, but being dead inside made me ache to complete the process.

I stared up at the ceiling and listened to the sounds of the house. I heard Dad laugh at something on the TV and Mom bang the kitchen cupboards. Soon I heard the microwave beeping and smelled the aroma of popcorn drifting down the hall. Sherlock was whining at my door but I didn't get up to let him in. Instead, I rolled over and turned off my bedroom light. Even if I didn't fall asleep for hours, I wouldn't have to risk talking to Mom or Dad or having Joe find me on Facebook.

The next morning I was already in the library when Aliya walked in.

"You'll never guess what happened!" she said.

I was sitting at a table in the back corner with my math books open. I was exhausted from not sleeping most of the night, but I tried to act energetic.

"What?"

"The police were at the park this morning. They had it blocked off with yellow tape and everything."

A zap of electricity shot up my spine.

"What park?"

"The one at the end of your street."

I tried not to react but I felt like throwing up. "Why?"

"I dunno. The bus driver said they found someone hanging there this morning."

"Dead?" I said. I didn't even have to fake my alarm. I mean, what if Sam and Ray didn't call the police and some kid accidentally hung himself on my rope? I hadn't meant to leave it there. My stomach heaved again.

Aliya shrugged. "I don't know. It sure is creepy though. Two hangings in one week. Mom's going to freak. Whenever she hears anything about suicide she loses it. And it's been like thirty years since her sister died."

I fiddled with the scarf at my neck. "I'm glad I didn't see it."

Aliya and I worked through a few math problems but it was hard to concentrate. I'd taken three painkillers but I could still feel my skull vibrating and the skin on my neck burning.

"What's up with the scarf anyway?" she finally asked.

"I woke up with a sore throat," I said.

"You're not trying to hide something, are you?"

She leaned over and tried to move the scarf with her finger, but I batted her hand away.

"Hands off."

"Did you ditch me for a boy last night? Maybe a boy named Kyle?" she teased.

I had no choice but to play along, so I smiled mysteriously. "You'll never know." But we both knew there was no way I'd ever end up with someone like Kyle and I wished for once that she'd just admit she was into him.

All day long rumours swirled around about what had been swinging on the end of that noose. Gisele said she heard it had been a dog. Mariam said her cousin texted her and told her it was a copycat hanging and the person was dressed like a vampire. Tyson said some gang had strung up a rival gang member as a warning to stay off their turf. Hearing all that nonsense was a relief because I knew if there was no real news then the police had simply taken down my empty noose.

It wasn't until the end of the day that I was completely relieved though. As I was walking home, I saw Sam and Ray surrounded by a gang of kids at the front of their school. My first instinct was to run away, but I knew that would look suspicious. So instead, I forced myself to stop, join the group, and listen.

"It was just hanging there, nothing was in it," Ray said.

"Did you see anyone?"

"No, the park was totally empty. We looked around but didn't see a thing," Sam said.

Kyle was in the crowd. I moved behind someone's head so he wouldn't see me.

"Maybe they ran off when you came along," someone suggested.

"I think it was just a prank," Ray said.

"But the police still came to check it out," Sam added.

"YOU called the police?" someone asked.

"Yeah. They took our names and asked some questions then they drove us home."

"Bet it won't be your last time in a cruiser," someone yelled, and everyone laughed.

When the crowd started to break up, I attached myself to a couple of other kids and drifted away. All I wanted was to get to my bedroom and be alone. By then my entire body was aching. It felt like I'd been in a car accident.

The first thing I did when I got home was take a long hot shower. Then I climbed into bed. I told Mom I thought I was coming down with the flu and stayed in my room for the next five days. I drank cough syrup and sucked throat lozenges just to make it look good. And when Mom brought me soft-boiled eggs and cups of hot soup, I smiled as gratefully as I could. But when she left, I fed them to Sherlock. For five days straight I ached to cry and fell deeper into the hole that was supposed to be my soul.

# ALIYA

This was one of the all-time creepiest weeks of my life. Seriously, it was like living in some freaky *Blair Witch Project* movie, with everyone going crazy for killing themselves suddenly. It all started with a guy at Thomas Jackson Secondary School. Everyone is saying that his suicide had to do with Halloween, like Halloween is a jinx. But that's ridiculous because I don't remember any other Halloweens when people decided to kill themselves in front of their schools.

I never gave it much thought before I found out about my aunt, but the last couple of days I've been trying to understand why someone would kill themselves. Apparently this guy was literally tormented to death by the kids at TJSS. Still, I can't imagine things being so bad I'd want to, like, *never* exist anymore. Sure it sucks being picked on all the time. Kids can be incredibly cruel and girls are the worst. I know from experience.

You know those girls who hate you for being something they aren't? In grade five the "in" girls stopped talking to me after our first art class. I was new that year and should have known better than to try too hard, but I sketched a picture of a baby giraffe and the art teacher went all giggly on me. She gushed about my fantastic eye and incredible attention to detail and, what's worse, she did it in front of everyone. I just thought it was a cute giraffe, but as soon as she started twittering like an excited bird, I saw trouble ahead.

Kira, the ringleader of the fashionistas, started scowling before class was even over. By lunch she'd publicly announced I had terrible taste in clothes and I should do something — anything — with my hair. By final bell, she'd found out I lived with just my mother and had spread the rumour that my father was a drunk, which is a complete lie.

It wasn't my fault I was good at art and I didn't do a single thing to make her hate me. It's not like I hated her because she was a fast runner or an Einstein at math. But Kira didn't like anyone doing anything better than she could. She made everyone stop talking to me and I mean *everyone*. By Christmas I had to play with the grade three kids because nobody in grade four or five would even look at me. There was one girl, Grace, who wanted to be my friend, I think. She was a lot nicer to me when Kira wasn't around anyway. I saw her at the YMCA one Saturday.

"I think you're a really good drawer," she said in the change room. We'd both just finished our swimming lessons.

"Thanks," I said.

"I wish I could draw like that."

"I'm sure you have some other talent," I offered.

"I play the piano. I'm in a recital next week!"

"That's cool." For the first time in weeks I was starting to feel hopeful about finally making a friend at school.

"Please don't tell Kira," she said sheepishly, as an afterthought.

"Don't worry. I won't."

"Is your dad really an alcoholic?"

"No. Kira just makes up lies about me. I never even met my father before."

"I didn't think so. She did that to another girl last year."

"What happened to her?"

"I don't know. She never came back after Christmas."

My heart plummeted, but I pulled it back up into my chest and took a steadying breath.

"Do you want to come over to our apartment sometime?"

"I don't think so," Grace said apologetically. "I'd like to, but if Kira ever found out I couldn't stand it."

I nodded and dried my hair, but I didn't say anything more. What was there to say? Grace finished putting on her clothes and slipped out of the change room. That was the beginning and the end of my friendship with Grace. We never spoke again. I didn't blame her, not even then. I mean, who'd want to associate with the school outcast? It just wasn't worth the risk. But it didn't make my life any easier either, knowing I'd almost had a friend.

Because of Kira, I was banned from using certain hallways or bathrooms in the school. If I did, watch out! The tormenting stepped up. I cried every day that year and it was the longest ten months of my life. Mom was ready to pull me from school altogether. But I got through it and when I got to junior high everything turned around. That horrible girl went to a different school and my classmates, even ones from my middle school who'd been part of the torment, started thinking I was cool because I was good at drawing cartoons of them. I'd take a sketchpad outside at lunch and draw a different person every day. I had kids lining up and buying me chocolate bars to draw them next. I mean, how crazy is that? I didn't change at all or do anything different, but everything around me changed.

I feel terrible for the guy who hanged himself. He's going to miss the rest of his life. Maybe he was having a tough year. Maybe he was facing another three years of torment, and I know that sounds like forever, but it would have ended. It always ends. Or it did for me anyway. I wonder if he can see how he's turned the city upside down and if he wishes he could change the ending to his life.

Mostly though, I've been thinking about his family. Can you imagine what it would be like if someone you loved killed themselves? I heard from my friend that he has a little sister. Think about how messed up she's going to be for the rest of her life. Just like my mom. Even though she doesn't realize it, Mom's still getting over her sister's suicide. I mean, I'm almost seventeen and she refuses to let me go to parties or sleepovers. She says she doesn't mean to suffocate me, but if I'm ten minutes late getting home from school she has that panicked look on her face. It breaks my heart to see her get so stressed out. But I hate it too. I sort of hate my aunt for putting my mom through this, even though I never even met the lady before. She was dead  before I came along.

It seems like such a waste to kill yourself. Even if everyone in the whole school told me to go kill myself the way they did to him, I still wouldn't. Maybe I'm just too stubborn. Anyhow, as if that guy's suicide wasn't creepy enough and the only thing everyone was talking about, a few nights later there was a copycat attempt in a park that I pass on my way to school. The police said someone probably got interrupted and that they're likely to try again sometime. One day at school I told Kyle that if I could just find that person I'd handcuff myself to them until they changed their mind.

"Do you have handcuffs?" he asked. I could tell he was in the mood to be a smartass. Sometimes he's really sweet and sensitive, but sometimes he just likes to make jokes about everything, and I thought this was one of those times.

"No, I don't have handcuffs," I said as I closed my locker. "It was just a figure of speech. But if I knew someone was thinking about killing themselves, I wouldn't leave their side for a single second until I'd made them realize life is full of too much possibility to throw it all away. And I'd make them come and talk to my mom about what it's like to be left behind, to lose someone you depended on being there for the rest of your life."

"I think if someone is determined to do themselves in they're going to find a way, no matter how hard you try to save them," Kyle said.

The bell went and everyone scattered to their classes.

"That's the most ridiculous thing I've ever heard," I said. "Some people just need to know they aren't alone."

I knew we had to finish our conversation quick or some teacher was going to see us in the hall and yell at us for not being in class. Still, what we were talking about was important.

"I think it's more complicated than that. Sometimes there's mental illness involved."

"What, are you, like, a suicide expert or something?" I asked.

"No. But sometimes on the news you hear about people killing themselves and they're, like, sick, in their heads."

"Could you ever kill yourself?" I asked as I glanced up and down the empty hall.

Kyle shook his head. "Not in a million years. Living is way too much fun. What about you?"

"Nope. Definitely not. Even if I was miserable I wouldn't be able to hurt the people I love. Think about it. If someone you love dies in an accident or gets cancer, that's one thing. It's sad, but there's nothing you can really do about it. But having someone you love take themselves away from you on purpose — you wouldn't know whether to feel sad or just downright pissed at them, and you'd always think there was something you should have done differently."

We saw the principal at the far end of the hall and she was heading our way. Her heels clicked on the tile floor.

"I gotta run. See you after school," Kyle said and sprinted in the opposite direction. I slipped around the corner and headed to my class too.

That night I took the bus home alone. Anna had been away sick for a few days. In fact, she'd been away since the day after she ditched me instead of coming over to work on our math together. It had been an emotional week and I was tired from not sleeping well. Every time I started to fall asleep, I'd see that guy from TJSS in a vampire costume hanging in front of his school, only as I got closer, I'd see Anna's face under the makeup. Then I'd startle and find my body covered in goosebumps. It seemed like a totally random image at first, but then it sort of made sense — maybe *Anna* tried to hang herself! I mean, stay with me here. Her grandparents were both killed in a freak accident less than two years ago, she's been moody lately, and she lives just down the street from the park where they found the noose hanging.

I hate to admit it, but I actually thought about calling the police. I mean, what if she was about to hang herself but got scared? I even went so far as to look up the tip line on the Internet, but then I couldn't go through with it. I know I have a crazy imagination and sometimes it takes control of me. I couldn't send the police over to Anna's house because she's been moody, ditched me one night, and missed a few days of school. If I was wrong, I wouldn't be able to face her ever again. Besides, it's totally insane to suspect Anna of wanting to kill herself. Anna has everything going for her. She's smart, pretty, and she's an awesome painter. To tell the truth, she's the first kid I ever met who could draw better than me. She lives in a rich neighbourhood and her parents still like each other, even though they've been married since high school or something. I doubt she's ever been teased, like, not even once. Everyone wants to be friends with Anna, especially Kyle. And Kyle is a total catch. He's definitely worth sticking around for.

I tried to put the thought completely out of my mind, but the next day at school my big mouth blurted it out.

"Do you think Anna's okay? I'm kind of worried about her?"

"She has the flu. I texted her last night to find out where she's been," Mariam said.

We were sitting at our regular table in the cafeteria, in the corner by the doors that lead to our part of the school.

"Besides the flu. Don't you think she's been acting a little odd lately," I said. I lowered my voice so the kids at the nearby tables couldn't hear me, which means Gisele and Mariam had to lean in close to hear above the noise.

"What are you getting at?" Gisele asked.

"I was just thinking about that copycat noose. It was in the park just down the street from Anna's house, and it was the same night she was supposed to come to my place but didn't show."

Mariam laughed. "It's a big city. Lots of people live near that park."

"Wait. I thought she was acting weird a while back too. Like I thought she might be pregnant or something," Gisele said.

I was glad someone was taking me seriously.

"But whatever it was, she seems to be over it now," Gisele continued.

"Me too. I thought she was being kinda spacey a few weeks ago, but I just figured it had to do with her grandparents' accident or something," Mariam said. She took a bite of her sandwich. "Besides, of everyone I know, Anna is the last person who'd would want to kill herself."

"You're probably right. I'm probably overreacting. But still, it's awfully suspicious. I mean, she said her mom was going to drop her off, then she said she forgot her math books and had to take a bus back home to get them."

"I think she's just complex," Kyle said. He'd joined the conversation late and was eating a plate of nachos.

"Whatever!" Gisele laughed. "If she had a rock-sized pimple on her nose, you'd think that was *complex* too."

That night I found the courage to ask Mom about her sister, even though I was pretty sure I was going to get shut down before I could find out anything useful. Still, I had to try. I hoped there'd be a clue, some detail that would make me feel better about whatever was going on with Anna. I waited until we were doing the dinner dishes so we wouldn't have to look at each other.

"Do you miss Helen?" I asked as I handed her a plate to dry. I know we're the only people left on the entire planet without a dishwasher, but the apartment only has a sink and, when we moved in, Mom said we could manage with just the two of us to clean up after.

She cleared her throat and I wasn't sure she heard me, but then she said: "I guess. I mean, yes, of course. It's been so long though."

"She was older than you, right?"

"Two years."

"What happened to her?"

"She got in with the wrong crowd at high school. She started skipping classes and smoking pot. That led to other things. It was the seventies and things were crazy. Then she started staying out all night. The police would bring her home sometimes. My parents flipped out. They didn't have a clue what to do. When they were teenagers, drinking beer and smoking cigarettes was considered wild. Eventually she just got so wrapped up in taking drugs, she got careless, I guess."

"What did she die of?"

"An overdose."

"Of what, though?"

"I don't know. Lots of things. Do we have to talk about this? It was almost thirty years ago."

"But you never talk about it. I still can't believe I didn't know you had a sister all this time. I mean, you don't have a picture of her anywhere. I've never even heard anyone mention her name, not once."

"I talk about her."

"You've NEVER talked about her when I've been around."

"No, it's usually when you're not there."

"But why?"

"My parents wouldn't allow it when I was in high school. It was something they were ashamed of. I guess I got used to not speaking her name."

"But it must have been pretty terrible to lose your sister and then not even be able to talk about her."

Mom stopped drying and looked at me.

"It was a nightmare. You have no idea. I can't even describe it. I don't think I was ever the same after that."

"Don't you think it would have helped to talk about it?"

"Yes and no. Some things are better left unsaid."

"It's wrong, if you ask me. If she'd died of leukemia or in a car accident, you'd have pictures of her on the wall. You would have named me after her or something. There'd be some sign she existed. But it's like you wish she was never alive in the first place."

"That's not true," Mom said. There was a sharp edge to her tone and I knew I should drop it.

"I'm just saying," I said quietly and let the rest of the sentence dissolve in my mouth.

# ANNA

It took me a few weeks to recover from my failed hanging. Not only did my back and neck ache for over two weeks, I was so shaken by what I'd almost done I found it hard to get back on track. In fact, I was so downhearted I almost forgot about the list I'd hidden in my math binder, between the cardboard insert and the vinyl cover. It was a list of all the ways someone could kill themselves. At least it was everything I could think of. It wasn't until I came downstairs one Saturday morning and saw Mom sitting on the couch that the memory choked me. Sherlock was warming her feet and she had my binder on her lap. Her hands were folded over it and she had a faraway look in her eyes.

"Mom?" I asked.

She turned to face me but she didn't say anything.

"Everything okay?" I asked again.

I was afraid to step any closer so I stayed at the threshold of the living room and watched the distance expand between us.

"I'm fine," she smiled absently.

She paused and although I wanted to flee, I waited for the ambush.

"I was just thinking about Christmas. Maybe we should shake it up a bit this year. Do something different. What do you think?"

The sweat that had been building on my forehead evaporated so quickly I felt faint.

"Sure, whatever you want. As long as we're all together." I tried not to stare at the binder but I had an overwhelming urge to rip it out of her hands.

"That's what I thought too, but your dad is so traditional."

I couldn't think of what to say so I stood as quietly as I could. Mom got lost in her thoughts again.

"So, um, did you need my binder for something?" I asked finally.

"No, sorry. Not at all. I just borrowed a piece of paper to start my shopping list."

She fluttered the list in the air and handed me the binder. I grabbed it and hugged it to my chest. Then I chastised myself for leaving it out in the first place.

"I have to study for a test," I said.

"I'm going to the mall later if you want to come," she called out as I padded down the hall to my bedroom.

"Sounds good," I called back to her, "let me know when you're leaving."

To be honest, I had no desire to go to the mall. There was nowhere I could go that was going to make me feel any better. In fact, I knew being at the mall would probably make me feel worse than just sitting in my room. But I was feeling too restless to be alone.

I sat down on my bed and found the small tear in the cover of my binder. I got a pair of tweezers and pulled the list free. I knew what was written there and didn't need to read it, but still, I unfolded the piece of paper.

## Ways to Kill Yourself

- ~~jumping from a bridge~~ (definitely afraid of heights)
- ~~getting hit by a moving truck~~ (can't take the chance of killing someone else)
- slashing wrists (not an option — thought of blood makes me pass out)
- carbon monoxide poisoning (not an option — access to a car and a garage problematic)
- gunshot to the head (not an option — access to a gun problematic)
- ~~hanging~~ (how did that TJSS guy do it?)
- drowning (still possible? maybe if water is cold?)
- overdose

It seemed like years had passed since I'd walked across suicide bridge, but it had only been four months. I glanced out my bedroom window at the snow falling. Even the botched hanging had receded. Panic clawed out from inside my chest and I lay down on my bed. I tucked my knees under my chin and tried to clear my mind. *What was wrong with me?* I wondered. *Why couldn't I just go through the motions of living like everyone else and act happy? Was everyone as miserable as me but a better actor? Did Aliya sometimes wish she could fall asleep and never wake up? Did Kyle ever want his brain to just shut up?* I shook the thought from my head and sat up again. I needed a distraction and turned on my laptop. Joe found me on Facebook within minutes.

"Do U ever study or R U, like, always on FB?" I asked him.

"Nice conversation starter," he quipped back.

"Sorry. How R U?"

"Fine. Did Mom tell U her big plan for Christmas?"

"Not really, what?"

"She wants to go on a cruise."

"Really?"

"Yeah, she thinks if we stay home all we're going to do is think about Granny and Gramps like last year."

I didn't know what to write back. I didn't want to think about Granny, or Gramps.

"U still there?" Joe wrote a minute later.

"Yeah, I'm here. Getting away would be good."

"She needs us to convince Dad."

"How?"

"You're his favourite. Don't U have any strategies?"

"Yeah, rite, I'm his favourite. Where does she want to go?"

"Alaska, but they don't run in winter."

*Too bad*, I thought when I pictured all that icy water slapping at the hull of a cruise ship.

"Where else?"

"The Caribbean, the Mediterranean, the South Pacific."

"Aren't cruises big $$$$?"

"Yeah, I was surprised too. But something down in the Caribbean is probably ok."

"It would be nice to be warm for a week."

"So talk to Dad."

"I'll see what I can do."

I'd never been on a ship before but I imagined it would be pretty easy to sneak onto the deck at night and slip over the railing. Once I was in the ocean there was no way I'd be able to swim to safety and nobody would be around to rescue me. In fact, it might be considered an accident and Mom and Dad would be spared the grief of knowing they'd raised a suicidal freak.

"Sweetie?" Mom knocked on my door and poked her head into my room.

Sherlock, who was lying beside my bed, raised his head hopefully and whacked his tail on the floor. The cat jumped off my bed.

"I'm going to the mall now. You still want to come?"

I slapped my hand over the list lying beside me.

*I have to stop being so careless*, I thought.

"Yeah, sure. Give me five minutes."

I logged off my computer, tucked the note back into its secret compartment, and joined Mom in the car. I almost got out again because the thought of being at the mall was overwhelming, but I forced myself to put on the seatbelt.

Because the snow was falling hard, traffic moved slowly and what should have been a ten-minute drive seemed to take forever. To make matters worse, the wipers were squeaking across the windshield and the heater was blasting so hot on my face that I started to feel claustrophobic. I closed the air vent and sighed.

"You sound tired," Mom said. She glanced over and offered me a sympathetic smile.

"It's just this time of year," I said.

"I know how you feel. Which brings me to Christmas. I think we should go on a cruise. Skip the tree, turkey, and trimmings. Spend a week lounging around a pool."

"Sounds good to me," I said. I knew she didn't want to bring up Granny and Gramps, but not saying their names didn't mean we weren't both thinking of them.

"We just have to convince Dad. I think he's worried about you. Maybe you could let him know you're all right with changing it up this year?"

"Sure, I'll talk to him."

"I have my eye on a trip already. It leaves December eighteenth."

I suddenly got what she was doing. She wanted us out of the country before the anniversary of the accident. Like we'd somehow avoid thinking about them if we were in a different place. Their faces loomed large in my mind. I still hated myself for not crying at their funerals.

"That's close. Can you book something so late?"

"I haven't actually called, but a lady at work booked the week before Christmas last year. She got a last-minute deal."

Mom and I split up at the entrance of the mall and agreed to meet at the food court in two hours. She headed to the department store to buy underwear and I wandered in the opposite direction. I still wasn't sure why I was at the mall. I knew there was no point buying new jeans or boots if I wasn't going to be around to wear them.

When I was thirteen, I loved shopping as much as I loved drawing. I tried to fill the nagging void inside by buying new T-shirts and hoodies. But those days were a distant memory. Instead of stopping to admire the window displays at my old favourite stores, I rushed past. The Christmas music and frenzied shoppers made me feel anxious. I wasn't sure I could stand another season of forced cheerfulness and togetherness, even on a cruise ship. That's when the urgency hit me with so much force I had to stop and lean against the railing to catch my breath. I looked down at people walking on the level below. Groups of teenagers moved in herds. Couples split up to go around them.

"Hey, you!"

Without even looking up, I knew it was Gisele. It was getting harder and harder to fake my regular self and even smiling drained me. But as I turned around I somehow managed to transform my expression.

"Hey, Gisele. Are you working today?"

"I always work Saturdays," she said in a tone that implied I was an idiot not to remember.

"I've got my days mixed up. I thought today was Sunday," I said apologetically.

Gisele leaned over the railing beside me. She was the kind of friend who didn't mind silence. Still, I knew I'd need to come up with something to say sooner or later.

"Have you started your Christmas shopping yet?" It was all I could think to ask.

"No," she snorted. "Everyone on my list gets wine glasses or bowls."

"Oh yeah," I said. She worked at a kitchen store.

"Listen, are you feeling okay? I mean is something bothering you? You've been really out of it lately. Ever since the party at the forks."

My stomach thumped and I scrambled for an explanation.

"It's not just me," she continued. "Everyone else has noticed too. Aliya, Mariam. Even Kyle said he saw you one day wandering down by the highway."

"I wasn't wandering by the highway," I said a little too defensively. "I was looking for a box of Joe's stuff that fell off the moving truck."

"Joe moved a year and a half ago."

"Geez, Gisele. What's with the interrogation? He took some more stuff over to his apartment and a box of linens fell off."

Our language arts teacher taught us that the key to creating a believable story was in providing believable details. I applied the same theory to my lies. A box of linens seemed much more believable than just a *box*.

Gisele raised her eyebrows. "A box of linens?"

"You know my mom. She's a shopaholic. There was a sale. She thought he needed matching towels."

Gisele didn't look at me. She kept watching the heads below.

"What do you *think* I was doing down there?"

"I don't have a clue. I don't get you much lately. You're sort of quiet. Not yourself."

I took a deep breath. I knew I'd have to pull out an Oscar-winning performance if I was going to convince her everything was okay.

"Listen, keep it to yourself, but my parents have been fighting a lot lately. I think they might be getting a divorce. They haven't been the same since, you know, since my grandparents' accident."

Gisele nodded knowingly. "Wow, that's rough. But still, I never would have expected your parents to split up."

I nodded and pressed my lips into a straight line. "Don't say anything. Okay?"

"Okay."

"Promise?"

"I promise. I always thought your parents were so cute together."

"I know. It totally sucks. That's why I've been, well, preoccupied lately."

Gisele looked at her watch and stood up straight again.

"Sorry. My break's over. I gotta get back. Catch you later, okay?"

"Sure thing," I said.

"Talk to me, you know, if you're feeling, like, sad or something."

"I will."

Mom arrived at the food court with a large bag in each hand. I was eating some fries and drinking a Coke, even though I wasn't really hungry. It just made me feel less awkward to be doing something with my hands while I waited.

"That's a lot of underwear," I said and nodded at the bags.

She laughed. "It's not all underwear. They had a sale on bed sets so I got Joe a new comforter and two new pillows. I thought we could drop them off on our way home."

She looked for my reaction and when I didn't give anything away she sat down and took a french fry from the carton on the table.

"Is that okay?" she asked. "It's not going to put a wrinkle in your plans or anything?"

"That's fine," I said. "I haven't got any plans."

I stood up and took a bag off the floor.

"You don't want the rest of these fries?" she asked.

I shook my head. "Help yourself." Then I picked up the second bag so she could walk and eat at the same time.

I hadn't been over suicide bridge since the previous summer and I could feel myself tensing up when we got within view of it. The memory of the heat that day was so out of place with the snowy scene outside the car, I felt disoriented. I distracted myself once we were on River Road by looking down the steep banks. The river had started to freeze along the edges. It usually didn't freeze over completely until late December, when the temperatures dropped low enough. If I walked out past the ice and jumped into the water, I reasoned, the shock of the cold would immobilize me and I'd have a chance at drowning. But I only had a couple more weeks, then I'd have to wait for the spring thaw.

Jumping in the river seemed so easy. I'd already managed to jump in the river once, so maybe my body wouldn't be too freaked out about being on the ice. Besides, there'd be no heights, no rigging ropes, no timing traffic. *How hard could it be to sneak across the ice?* I asked myself. Then I remembered the boy who'd shot his face off, but somehow managed to survive. He was on the same talk show as the legless girl. He'd been so afraid to come out of the closet to his parents that he decided to take his father's rifle to his head. If you could screw up killing yourself with a gun, you could probably screw up anything. Still, I was starting to feel more desperate as the days went by and I woke up yet another morning to that hollow, nagging feeling that my life was a lie, that I didn't belong to any of it.

————

Mom and Dad had a Sunday ritual of going downtown for eggs Benedict at their favourite bistro. Or rather, Mom had a thing for eggs Benedict and Dad had to make it up to her for being away so much for work. So even though it was snowing hard and Dad tried to protest, Mom insisted they go.

"It's our time together. We deserve it," she said.

He kissed her and rattled his car keys.

I knew she just wanted some dedicated face time to talk about the Christmas cruise, but I didn't let on. I knew if I had the house to myself, there wouldn't be anyone around to ask questions about why I was going for a walk on such a miserable morning. Another opportunity might not come up again before Christmas, or the cruise, whichever came first.

I watched out the bay window until their car turned at the end of our street, then I bundled up and headed out the door. It had been snowing since before dawn so the streets were a mess and every time a car drove by it threw slush across the sidewalk. I pulled the hood of my jacket up over my head and trudged through the wind. Icy pellets stung my face so I looked at my feet, except at intersections where I glanced up to get my bearings and check the traffic. I didn't want to get plowed over by a car.

I had the sidewalk to myself and punctured fresh wounds in the snow with my boots. As a child I would have found satisfaction in breaking trail, but small pleasures like that had been eluding me for years.

I knew exactly where I wanted to join the river — down at the forks where I'd dragged myself out earlier in the fall. It was the only level place I'd be able to walk out onto the ice. I turned onto the bike trail at the top of River Road and headed down into the steep ravine. It was slow going since the path was covered in ice and the snow was falling so hard I could barely see. I'd ridden the length of the city along the bike trail with Dad before, winding beside the river all the way. In the summer the trails were busy, but I could tell nobody had ventured down all morning.

When I got to the bottom of the riverbank, I looked upriver, then down. Ice had formed ten or fifteen feet out and the water beyond that was black, but not still. The gusting wind tormented the surface into a frenzy of choppy waves and drove prickles of ice into my face. Other than the tree branches moaning in the wind, everything was quiet. I leaned down and dug a stone out of the snow. Then I threw it onto the ice. It bounced twice before slipping quietly over the edge. The ice was thicker than it looked, which was good. If I fell through near the bank, I'd be able to touch bottom and would just end up with wet, frozen legs on the walk home.

As I climbed down the last few feet to the edge of the river, my feet slipped. I had to scramble to get standing again.

I put one foot on the ice to test it. There wasn't a sound — not a crack, not a snap. I put my whole weight on that foot and waited, then slid my other foot to the front. I transferred my weight slowly. A raven screeched from the trees behind me but I didn't turn to look. It seemed fitting that there would be only the one witness. The farther out I got the smoother the ice was, and twice I had to stop to catch my balance. The smell of the cold, black water filled my head, but I refused to think of anything more than taking the next step. When I got to the edge, with one step left, I hesitated.

*Could I really do this?* I wondered. But I knew it wasn't the time to stop and think. Thinking always got me in trouble. *Just one more baby step*, I told myself. My pulse sputtered and I felt my body pulling back. My mind though, it was in a completely different mode. It was excited, edgy, and the contrast to the sudden drag in my feet made me feel like I was going to topple over headfirst. I was standing about fifteen feet from the bank of the river, trying to convince my feet to take that one last step, when the ice gave out under me and I plunged into the icy river.

I gasped at the shock of the cold. I had meant to sink silently to the bottom and not struggle, but again my body took control and my arms started flailing. My lungs struggled to breathe and my arms struggled to keep my head above the water. Then I felt the weight of my wet boots sucking me down and I cheered for the water, begged it to pull harder, faster. You know how they say your life flashes before your eyes when you are about to die? Well, that's not what happened to me. What I saw was my grandparents trapped in their car the day they died and the cold water rising up around them. I saw the panic on my grandmother's face and I imagined her screaming and calling for help. I saw my grandfather trying to break a window or open a door, but without any luck. I felt their intense fear, followed by a flash of calm, and that's when I knew they were so close I could touch them if I just reached out my hand.

"God almighty, lady! Grab my hand!"

The voice was impossibly near and even though I didn't mean to reach out, I swear I didn't, a hand found mine and pulled against the force of the river. It pulled and pulled and I felt like I was caught in that tug-of-war for hours, wondering who was going to win. In the end *he* won, the homeless guy who'd been tucked up in the undergrowth in his makeshift shelter when he heard a splash, a scream, and a cry for help. Or so he told the police when they arrived on the scene to wrap us both in emergency blankets and drag us to their cruiser.

The car heater was on full blast, but still, I shivered so hard my muscles screamed in pain.

"We've got the ambulance on the way," the police officer said over the back seat.

"I'm fine. Hardly even got my arm wet," the homeless man said. "This young lady though, she's shaking something terrible. She needs to get out of those clothes."

"I'm fine," I managed to gasp through my chattering teeth. I just wanted to go home and crawl into bed. The homeless man smelled of smoke and sweat and I was embarrassed to see a small crowd gathering outside the car. *Why on earth were so many people out on such a terrible day?* I wondered.

When the ambulance turned down River Road, the police officer stepped out of the car and moved the onlookers away. The homeless man turned to me.

"If you don't mind me asking, what the hell were you doing down there?"

The skin on his face was red and cracked and his two front teeth were missing.

"I dropped my ring … and it landed … out on the ice. I was just trying … to get it back…."

"It's not what it looked like to me. I mean, I'm no expert, but —"

I cut him off. "It … it was my … grandmother's…. She died …"

It was true, I did get my grandmother's wedding ring when she died, but it was safely tucked away in my bedroom. I shivered and watched while he decided whether to believe me or not.

"I'm sorry to hear about your grandmother," he said warily. "But next time just let it go. You almost got yourself killed. No ring is worth dying for."

I nodded through my shivering.

He pulled off one of his ragged gloves and held out his left hand. It was covered in dirt and sores. On his ring finger there was a gold band.

"This here is all I got left of my wife. She died of cancer ten years ago. Love of my life. Next to my cellphone it's all I got of value in this entire world, and I wouldn't risk my life for it, no matter what."

He pulled the glove back over his hand and opened the door. Before he left he looked hard at me and said, "You take care of yourself. You got your whole life ahead of you and you might not be so lucky next time."

Then I passed out.

I don't know if it was the cold or the shivering, or maybe just the disappointment, but a comfortable blackness took over. I remember thinking *maybe I did it after all,* and then there was nothing. Nothing, that is, until I woke up in a hospital, wrapped in hot blankets.

"She's going to be fine. She's just in a bit of shock. We've got her temperature back up to normal. Her heartbeat and breathing are strong." It was a doctor talking to my parents. "The police said a man pulled her out just before she went under. They're taking his statement now."

The face of the homeless man came to me and I hoped, in a sleepy, vague way, that he wouldn't blow my cover.

The next time I woke up, Mom was sitting beside me, watching me.

"Anna? Sweetie? How do you feel?"

"Tired," I managed to say. I closed my eyes again. I couldn't stand to see the worry on her face.

She didn't say anything more, but I knew I wouldn't be so lucky the next time I opened my eyes. Eventually, I knew, I'd have to talk about what had happened.

"What were you doing down there in the first place?" my father asked when we were back home. I was tucked into my bed sipping hot chocolate, wishing everyone would go away, but accepting my punishment as patiently as I could. Sherlock was lying at the foot of my bed by the hearing vent. He hates the cold.

"Taking pictures for my media class. We have to do a photo journalism project and I thought I'd do it on the river."

"But why did you go out on the ice?"

"I was on the bank and I slipped. The camera, like, skidded across the ice. I thought I could reach it okay, but I think it went in the river when I did."

"The police said something about you losing Granny's ring," Mom said.

Damn. I'd forgotten about the ring and now I had to toss out a perfectly good camera as well. I turned to look out the window. I couldn't look her in the face and see all that worry pooling there.

"It must have come off when that guy pulled me up."

"I'm sorry, sweetheart. I know how much that ring meant to you."

I didn't know which was worse, the sympathy or the worry. I put my mug of hot chocolate on the table beside my bed. "I think I'm going to sleep now," I said. "I'm really tired."

"Of course," Mom said, and she and Dad turned off the light and left.

When I heard them down in the living room, I snuck out of my bed, over to my desk, and took out my digital camera. I tucked it into my school bag so I could dump it in a garbage can on the way to school. It had been a birthday present and I hated to throw it out, but I couldn't have it showing up and prompting questions either. Next I went to my dresser and took Granny's ring out of my jewellery box. It felt heavy in my hand. Sherlock didn't even lift his head but his eyes followed me across the room. I lifted the heating vent out of the floor, reached my arm as far as I could down the duct, and dropped the ring.

# ANNA'S MOM

Our meals were just being delivered when my phone rang. I assumed it was going to be Anna telling us she made plans with one of her friends or asking us to pick something up on the way home, but it was the police. The blood drained out of my face so fast when I heard them say Anna's name, I would have been camouflaged if I'd been outside in the snowstorm. The next few hours are still a blur. I can't quite sort out the order of events, but I remember the police saying they were taking Anna by ambulance to South River Hospital. I also remember my husband watching me from across the table while he tried to figure out what was wrong.

"Who is it? What are they saying? What's going on?" He spoke louder with each question.

I waved my hand for him to be quiet, but he couldn't stop the stream of questions.

"Is it Joe? Anna? It's Anna? Is she okay? Where is she? Who are you talking to?"

I don't know if it's just my memory, but everyone in the restaurant seemed to freeze and the silence was painful. I stood up and turned my back to the room for privacy.

I plugged one ear with my finger and started repeating the information.

"South River Hospital. Emergency. Five minutes. Anna. Yes. Sixteen. River. Hypothermic. Yes. My husband and I. Yes. Right now."

When the police officer hung up, I ripped my coat from the back of the chair. I didn't even tell my husband to follow, I just knew he would. The waitress opened the door so we could get outside faster and asked if we needed a ride, if we were safe to drive. I nodded without even offering to pay for our untouched meals. We ran to the car. My husband shouted questions at me the whole way, but I didn't have the mental capacity to talk and think at the same time so I didn't say a word.

By the time we arrived at the hospital, Anna was stable. She was unconscious but they assured us, with great confidence, that she was going to be fine. She'd been awake and alert until the ambulance arrived and probably passed out as much from the shock as anything.

When my husband went to sit with her, I called Joe to tell him what had happened. I promised to update him in a couple of hours and assured him a final time, the way the doctor assured us, that she was going to be okay. A police officer waited nearby until I hung up, then asked to talk to me. We went and sat in a deserted corner of the waiting room. I listened while he told me what they'd pieced together about the morning. He told me some of what the homeless man had said in his statement. Then he asked if there was any chance Anna might have been trying to commit suicide. The question staggered me. Images of her life, of my life with her in it, flashed through my mind.

"Suicide? Anna? Definitely not. I'm sure there's some sort of explanation. She's a teenager so she has her bad days, but otherwise she's completely normal. Well-adjusted. She has friends. She excels in her art program. She gets good grades in her other classes. She's happy and outgoing. She's a joy to be around. She's always been special."

I didn't mean to sound offended, but there must have been an edge to my voice because the police officer apologized as soon as I stopped talking.

"It's a routine question. I'm sorry if I upset you," he said and closed his notebook.

"This man, who saved her, do you know his name? Do you know where he lives?"

Everything swirled in my mind and my vision faltered while I tried to grasp hold of the moment. Later I thought of ten other questions I wished I'd asked, but at the time I was focused only on the facts.

"The gentleman who rescued her is living in a makeshift shelter along the riverbank, by the forks."

"I have to find him and thank him. He saved my daughter's life." I choked on the word *life* and broke down. Tears streamed down my face and I hid my head in my hands. The thought that I almost lost my daughter flooded me with so much fear, I couldn't regain my composure. I couldn't even look up when the officer left the room.

"We'll do our best to locate him for you, ma'am," the police officer said. He put his hand on my shoulder while I shuddered and gasped for air. "In the meantime, you take care of yourself. And your daughter. She's one lucky girl."

Lucky. Yes, I knew she was lucky, that I was lucky, and I was more thankful than I'd ever been. In that moment I would have traded everything I owned or had ever owned, everything I would *ever* own, to guarantee my daughter, my Anna, would always be safe. In one fast-framed moment, my perspective collapsed and nothing was important except that I had been spared the worst possible nightmare. The realization jolted me second by second, as if I'd just drunk too many espressos, and as I walked down the hospital corridor reality reinvented itself over and over until, by the time I arrived at Anna's bedside, I'd grown accustomed to the idea that she was, after all the terror, safe and alive. Somehow I'd gone from a normal weekend morning to the worst moment of my life and on to relief. The roller-coaster ride left me feeling exhausted.

When we left the hospital that afternoon, I was overwhelmed with the memory of taking Anna home from the very same hospital as a newborn, and I wished suddenly for the days when we could keep her within reach, guarantee her safety twenty-four-seven. I wished there was a car seat we could strap her in that would protect her, even into adulthood. I didn't need my business degree to calculate that the value of my life without Anna, without either of my children, would be nothing.

We settled her into bed and I wanted to stay with her for the rest of the evening, but I could see all our fussing was annoying her. I knew it was time to clear out and give her the time she needed to process the day, but I couldn't get the conversation with the police officer out of my head either.

"I still don't understand what you were doing down at the river on such a terrible day," my husband said finally.

I studied her reaction.

"I'm doing a project on the river for my media class. I wanted to get pictures of it freezing over. But my hands were

DETACHED

so cold I dropped the camera and it fell on the ice. I thought I could get it back. I'm sorry. It was a stupid thing to do."

I sighed. It was a perfectly reasonable explanation. Anna always invested a lot into her school work, especially where art was involved.

"We're just thankful you're safe," I said.

"I'm sorry about losing the camera too."

"It's just a camera. Dad can pick up another tomorrow."

"Sure I can," my husband said. "It's easily replaced."

"The police officer said something about Granny's ring?" I said. I was sitting on the edge of the bed, rubbing Anna's leg through the comforter.

Anna paused and examined her hand.

"I was wearing it this morning. It must come off when that man pulled me out of the water."

I could see tears pooling in Anna's eyes.

"I'm sorry, sweetheart." I leaned over and gave her a hug. "I know how much that ring meant to you."

Anna wiped her eyes and laid her head back on her pillow.

"You ready to go to sleep?"

Anna nodded and my husband stood up. He put his hands on my shoulders.

"We'll be downstairs. Call out if you need anything," he said, and guided me toward the door. I knew if he didn't make me leave I'd spend the night watching Anna sleep, and that wouldn't do anyone any good.

Anna smiled to let us know she appreciated the space.

We turned the TV on but kept the volume low. I don't think either of us knew what we were watching. I know I was too busy listening for sounds from Anna's room. I ached for her to call out, to need one of us back at her side the way she did when she was a little girl with the flu. But she was, after all, an independent sixteen-year-old. When my shoulders started to tremble, my husband took my hand and squeezed.

"It's okay," he said. "She's safe and sound and upstairs asleep."

"I couldn't have survived if we'd lost her to that awful river," I said, then burst into tears. We continued to stare at the television, but we didn't talk. Neither of us wanted to consider the what-ifs, not this time. At one point I thought I heard Anna moving upstairs, but I assumed it was Sherlock and did my best not to investigate.

# ANNA

I was beginning to think maybe I was one of those suicide attempters who did it for attention, as a cry for help. Part of me wondered if I really didn't want to die and that's why I couldn't find the perfect suicide, but then I laughed out loud at myself.

"What's so funny?" Mariam asked. We were sitting together at a table in the cafeteria.

"I was just thinking about something Joe said this morning."

"What?"

"Inside joke about his roommate."

Mariam went back to eating her lunch and I played with the straw in my chocolate milk.

"Hey, guess what was on the radio this morning?" she said.

"Dunno."

"The mayor is going to give that guy an award, the keys to the city or something, for saving you."

I grunted. The homeless guy had been in the news non-stop since he ruined my life — or my death, I should say. The story of my rescue, which was torture to hear told over and over again, reminded me I was a failure. I couldn't even look at myself. When I was alone in my room I put a sweater over the mirror, and when I was in the bathroom I brushed my teeth with my eyes closed.

The media interest lasted almost until Christmas, then someone had the bright idea of setting up a trust fund in the guy's name so people could donate money to his future instead of buying their kids more plastic junk. Just when that story started to die down, some rich people who were touched by his bravery offered him a rent-free apartment above their garage. Then someone who owned a printing press offered him a job, and a dentist offered to fix his teeth for free. It was like the entire city went nuts for the guy and tried to outdo the previous good deed. There was even a new parkette named after him. Every time I saw his face on the news I wanted to die more than I ever had before I was pulled out of that damn river. My parents even made a statement to the media, thanking him publicly for risking his life to save me, and forced me to stand beside them outside our house, which meant my stupid face was on the news for two days straight. My dad was also reluctant, but my mom insisted. I look okay in real life, more or less, but I look hideous on TV, and seeing myself on our big-screen television didn't do anything to make me feel better about myself. I mean, not a single thing. All I could think was that if only we'd been on a cruise, I would have escaped the torture. But after my near-death experience my parents decided to stay put. I wouldn't have been surprised if Joe hated me too, for ruining his chance to get away for Christmas.

"Well, I think it's nice. I mean, he could have fallen in too and you both would have drowned. He's a hero and you don't even seem grateful," Mariam said.

"It's not that. It's just sort of, well, embarrassing. I wish everyone would forget about it."

Sam, Ray, and Kyle walked past our table and Mariam stopped talking to watch.

"Sam is so hot," she said dreamily. She loved that we shared a cafeteria and gym with the regular high school. She said it gave her more choices in guys.

"Sam's a pig," I said.

"He just likes to pretend," Mariam said defensively.

"Whatever," I muttered to myself.

Kyle glanced over and smiled at me. I nodded back.

"You going to eat that pizza?" Mariam asked when the boys disappeared.

I looked down and noticed I hadn't touched it, not a single slice of pepperoni.

"Help yourself," I said and pushed my plate across the table. Mariam didn't seem to mind that it was cold. She ate and talked at the same time.

"Ray's having a party at his house this weekend. He's turning eighteen. Sam told me we should stop by. Dad said I can take the car if you want a ride."

"Sure," I said, even though I knew I'd find a last-minute excuse to bail. Sometimes I wondered why my friends bothered with me at all, especially since the party at the forks.

The bell rang and Mariam stood up. "Ask Aliya if she can come too," she said before trotting off in the direction Sam had gone.

"Sure thing," I called out, even though I knew there was no way Aliya's mother would let her go to Ray's party. I also knew that if she slept over, my parents wouldn't let us go either. Aliya's mother had made it clear on several occasions that she didn't approve of drinking under age.

I forgot all about the party until Mariam called Saturday afternoon.

"I'll pick you up at ten," she said.

"I was just about to call you, actually. I don't think I can go. I've got a wicked headache."

"So take a pill. I'll be there at ten."

She hung up before I could protest again. The idea of a house full of drunk people was unbearable and yet I knew Mariam wasn't going to let it drop. I curled into a question mark on my bed. I had six hours to come up with a foolproof excuse and my brain felt too tired to think. I felt my math binder calling attention to itself, as if it was daring me to unfold that list I'd made, the one that I'd opened and closed so many times the paper was as soft as felt. But I knew there was only one option left — one that I'd be able to face anyhow. That's when it struck me that an overdose might work after all, it just required some research.

I sat up and logged on to my laptop. I typed "overdose" into the web browser and felt a surge of excitement when so many results popped up. I skipped over the sites that talked about preventing teen suicide and opened a page that looked promising, until I realized it was full of statistics about the rates and types of suicides. Finally I started to find bits of useful information, like, boys more often succeed than girls; the wrong dose of cough syrup could slow down a person's breathing; teenagers sometimes overdose when they drink too much looking for a high. *How much is too much?* I wondered. Why didn't they just spell it out for me?

"Anna, dinner's ready," Mom called from the kitchen.

I bookmarked several sites then went downstairs.

After dinner I read about barbiturates and opium and wondered where I was going to find enough prescription meds to kill myself. Then I read about codeine. Just reading the word relaxed me.

"Codeine." I said it out loud. It sounded like the name of one of the cool boys at school. Codeine was used to control extreme pain, such as after a trauma. Codeine was like the name of my new best friend.

I was still scrolling through websites when the doorbell rang. Sherlock perked up his ears and I looked at the clock at the bottom of my computer screen. Somehow I'd lost track of time.

"Anna!" Dad called. "Mariam and Gisele are here."

I opened my bedroom door. "Send them up. I'm still getting ready."

I slapped my laptop closed and dumped it on the bed. Then I started pulling jeans out of my closet. Gisele and Mariam knocked quickly then walked in.

"Hey, Sherlock," Gisele said and stopped to scratch his ears.

"You're not ready?" Mariam asked.

"I'm just trying to decide. Which ones?" I held up two pairs of jeans.

They both pointed to the pair in my left hand so I dropped my track pants and pulled them on. Then I reached blindly into the closet and grabbed a shirt.

"Okay, let's go," I said.

"Don't you even want to, like, brush your hair or something?" Gisele asked. She looked around the room. "Why do you have your mirror covered up?"

"It reflects the outside light at night and keeps me awake."

I grabbed my brush but I didn't dare look at myself. A few quick pulls and I said, "This is as good as it gets. I call shotgun." I wanted to get them out of my room and away from my laptop as quickly as possible.

Mom and Dad were sitting together on the couch in the living room when we walked through to leave.

"We're going to a party. I won't be too late."

"No drinking and driving," Dad reminded.

"Absolutely not," Mariam said. "We're too young to drink."

Dad looked over his glasses at her to see if she was for real.

"I'll watch she doesn't have anything," I said.

Dad nodded his satisfaction and we said goodbye. On the way through the entrance, I was sure to look at my feet and not in the mirrored closet door. When we got in the car, Gisele leaned forward while Mariam buckled herself in.

"It looks like your parents are getting along again," Gisele said.

"Yeah, I guess it was a false alarm." I reached forward and turned on the radio so I wouldn't have to say anything more.

Ray's street was jammed with parked cars and even from three blocks away we could hear the music blaring.

"The police are going to show up for sure," Gisele said nervously.

"Maybe we shouldn't go in," I added hopefully.

"It's fine," Mariam said. "Sam says he does this every year. His neighbours are cool. They don't complain."

Gisele and I trailed behind while Mariam charged along the icy sidewalk.

"What's with that?" I asked when we got to Ray's house.

Instead of steps leading up to the front door, there was a wooden ramp.

"Ray's dad had an accident at work. He broke both his legs and, like, fractured his spine or something. He was in the hospital for a couple of months. But he's home now," Mariam said.

"Ray's parents are here?" I asked, panicked.

"Yeah, but it's no big deal. They let him have people over all the time."

There were a few kids huddled in the front yard smoking, and a couple more kids were standing on the porch talking. When we walked up the ramp and through the front door, nobody seemed to mind that we didn't knock.

The house was packed and the air was thick and sweaty. There were kids from our school who I knew and kids I'd never seen. I hoped nobody recognized me as the river-rescue girl. I hated having to fake enthusiasm for having my life saved by a homeless dude.

The bottom floor was standing room only and we had to squeeze through the crowd to get to the dining room, where everyone had dumped their coats in a huge pile on the table.

"C'mon," Mariam said. "The keg's on the back deck."

We squeezed through the kitchen and out the sliding-glass door. Ray and Sam were there, filling plastic cups with beer. Sam handed one to me and smiled.

"Hey, Anna. Kyle's around somewhere. He was in the living room last I saw." Sam winked at Mariam and they both laughed.

"Okay, thanks," I said and took a gulp of beer. It was as cold as the river.

Mariam struck up a conversation with Sam, and Gisele started talking to Ray. I drifted back inside because it was too cold to make small talk.

With so many people crammed into one small house it was hard to decide where to go, and I wondered where Ray's parents were hiding. I lapped the bottom floor. The living room was full of jostling, dancing bodies, but I didn't see Kyle. I nodded hello to kids from school and drank my beer. Another lap and I could see Gisele and Mariam were still in deep conversation, shivering in their shirts on the back deck. I made my way to the front entrance.

"Hey, Anna!" I heard someone call out. It was Farah, standing partway up the stairs. She motioned for me to join her. I headed up and was grateful to be above the people who kept bumping me. One leg of my jeans was already wet with beer.

"What's up?" I yelled over the pounding music.

"Cool party!" Farah said.

I wasn't sure she heard my original question.

"Hey," she shouted at me again. "Did Aliya come?"

"She wasn't allowed," I shouted back. "I came with Mariam and Gisele."

"Do you know where Ray's parents are?" I asked, loudly, next to Farah's ear.

"I heard someone say they were upstairs in their bedroom. But someone else said they were gone for the weekend and that Ray's just saying they're home so nobody does anything stupid."

"Good thinking," I said and then took another gulp of beer. It didn't really matter either way to me if they were there or not. I wasn't going to talk to them.

Kyle walked past the staircase and looked up. He smiled and waved.

"Come dance," he shouted at me.

Farah nudged me, but the thought of being in the living room with a crowd of b-boys and ballerinas terrified me. I hadn't been kidding when I told Kyle I had three left feet. Then I felt that surge in the pit of my stomach and I wished for once I could just chug back my beer and let myself have fun. I knew I should be happy Kyle asked me to dance. I hated being such a bore.

Kyle was still at the bottom of the stairs, looking up expectantly.

I dug deep for a smile, then shouted down at him, "Just got to hit the bathroom first."

I touched my plastic glass against Farah's then headed the rest of the way up the stairs. I found the bathroom and locked myself in. It wasn't as hot and loud in there, and I was relieved to be alone for a few minutes. I looked around. There were metal railings beside the toilet and in the bathtub.

*Ray's father must have been seriously injured*, I thought. *He must have been in a lot of pain.* My mind ticked over. *He might still be in a lot of pain.* I looked down at the sink while I opened the medicine cabinet. Inside was a row of prescription bottles lined up like football players. I pulled the bottles down one at a time and read the labels. Jackpot. One was filled with codeine. I pressed down and twisted off the cap, then shook the pills into my hand. I knew I couldn't take them all so I pocketed a few and put the bottle back.

"You want to hurry up in there?" Someone knocked on the door.

"Just a minute," I called out and flushed the toilet.

I went back downstairs and lapped the bottom floor again. Gisele and Mariam were still talking to the boys, but they'd moved inside to the kitchen. I was surprised they lasted in the cold as long as they did.

"Hey, Anna, where'd you go?" Mariam asked when she saw me.

"Just talking to people," I said, then moved on. I wasn't in the mood for being the odd one out. I wondered how much longer before I'd be able to bail.

When I couldn't stand being inside another minute, I fought my way to the dining room and dug around until I found my coat. Then I slipped out to the front porch. I pulled my coat tight around my neck and leaned over the railing. The fresh air settled the panic in my chest a bit. Everyone had gone back inside and I was relieved to be alone again.

"Here you are," Kyle said when he found me a few minutes later.

"Hey," I said. "It's so hot and crowded in there. I was having a hard time breathing."

"Yeah, Ray has wicked parties. But it can get to be a bit much."

When I didn't say anything, Kyle leaned over the railing to look at me. I could smell the beer on his breath.

"Everything okay?" he asked.

"I've had a headache all day and it's getting late. I guess I'm ready to go home soon."

"You want me to take you?"

"You have a car?"

"Sam drove here, but he'll be too wasted to drive home. I think that's why he brings me along in the first place."

"Brothers," I snorted.

"So you want a ride? I don't mind and I haven't even had a whole beer." He laughed. "And that was three hours ago."

I thought about being alone in a car with Kyle and my first thought was, like, no way in hell. I was afraid he'd want to talk about my bridge painting or, worse, the river incident or the day he saw me down by the highway. I was afraid I'd say one wrong thing and he'd put it all together and attempt his own rescue of a lost soul. But then I thought about how long it would be before Mariam would be ready to go.

"I could probably walk."

"It's almost midnight. You can't walk home by yourself. Especially in this cold. I'll give you a ride."

"You really don't mind?"

"No worries," he said and flashed me a smile with his perfect white teeth. "The car's over here. C'mon."

I followed him, then paused.

"When you get back, can you tell Mariam you gave me a ride home? Otherwise she'll be pissed I ditched her."

"Absolutely," he said and unlocked the door. "You live over by Melborn and Ellington, right?"

"Just past that park with the, uh, baseball diamond," I said.

It was awkward at first being alone in the car with Kyle and I searched for something to say.

"Too bad Aliya couldn't come," I finally said.

"Yeah, her mother's, like, way beyond strict."

Kyle was actually pretty easy to be with. He didn't ask a bazillion dumb questions to make me talk and he didn't rattle on about himself. He slowed down when we drove by the park. My hands started to sweat and I had an urge to roll down the window, but then I realized he just didn't know which street to turn onto.

"Next right," I said and he pulled down our street.

"That house there with the blue bins out already. My dad takes his recycling very seriously."

"We all have to do our part," he said and smiled.

I climbed out of the car, then put my head back inside. The warm air poured over my face.

"Thanks for the ride. Don't let Mariam drink. She has to drive."

"No worries. I have to keep an eye on Sam anyway, and she's never too far away."

After the party at Ray's, I actively scouted out new parties and found ways to get invited. Sometimes it would be through a friend of a friend or sometimes I'd muster the courage to talk to whoever was holding the party. If I saw them in the hall or the cafeteria, or in front of the school, I'd call out "see you tonight" and shout some wild animal sound, like "woot woot." If I didn't get a strange look, I considered it an invitation, of sorts.

My parents seemed secretly pleased by my new social life.

"You're going out again?" my dad said one night.

Then my mother countered with something like, "It's the age. I remember going through the same thing when I was sixteen."

My friends were happy about the new social me too. We texted and Facebook messaged constantly about where the party was going to be and when and how we'd get there. Mostly Mariam drove because she had a licence and could get a car, or sometimes we'd convince Kyle to take us along with him and Sam. But no matter how exciting it was for my friends or my parents, for me it was just a mission, a means to an end. I figured if I took a few pills from medicine cabinets here and there, it wouldn't take long to have, like, a bowlful of them. That's how I imagined it anyway, a crystal dish full of little coloured candies. Once I had enough, I planned to wash them down with a bottle or two of cough syrup and fall into a long, deep forever sleep. No pain, no trauma, nobody to rescue me. I couldn't believe I didn't consider it earlier.

I was surprised how many opportunities I found for stealing prescription codeine. It was like someone or something was cooperating with me finally. Maybe God figured I deserved to die after all. Like, when Farah complained to me during class one day that her deadbeat uncle had moved into their house and that he was on welfare because of chronic back pain, I found a way to get myself invited over. It didn't take long to find out which room he slept in and nobody seemed suspicious when I excused myself during dinner to go to the bathroom. Instead I snuck into his room, pocketed a few of his pills, then doubled back to flush the toilet before heading to the table again. The day after Aliya's mother had to have a double root canal, I just happened to be at her apartment studying. The pills were on the kitchen counter so it took some fancy manoeuvring to sneak the bottle into my pocket and then return it, but my patience paid off. I wasn't sure how many pills I needed, but I wasn't taking any chances, I was going to get it right. Five was my number. There wasn't going to be a sixth time lucky for me.

When Mom and Dad announced they were going away for a weekend to celebrate their anniversary, I knew it was the perfect opportunity. I'd have the house to myself for two days so nobody would find me passed out and rush me to the hospital for a dramatic rescue. I pulled my secret stash from its hiding spot and looked at the collection of variously coloured pills. They reminded me of Skittles. I was sure I had enough. All I had left to do was hit a couple of pharmacies and get some cough syrup. I even knew which brand to buy. Normally I hated the taste of cough syrup, but I was sure I could chug a couple of bottles if I tried hard enough.

I was anxious the week before my parents went away. I worried that something would happen and they'd change their plans or they'd get cold feet and ask Joe to spend the weekend with me. I was on my best behaviour for that final stretch and I covered my anxiety with upbeat smiles. I promised to have Gisele spend the nights so I wouldn't be alone.

"I bought frozen pizzas and lots of snacks. Maybe you two can watch something on Netflix. No parties, though," Mom said. "Oh, and I told the Rodman's you'd be here alone and to keep an eye on the place."

"Don't worry. I won't let anyone but Gisele come over. She'll be here in about an hour. Her mother's going to pick her up in the morning and take her to work, then drop her back at dinner."

"We'll have the cellphone with us the whole time. Don't be afraid to call if you need to. We're only two hours away," Dad said. They were packing the car and reminding me to feed Sherlock, clean the kitty litter, and all the other stuff I'd being doing since I was ten.

"I can always call Joe. Not that anything is going to go wrong," I assured them.

"Do you want me to ask him to drop over?"

"We'll be fine, Mom. Sherlock's here, and besides, I have an afternoon shift at the store so I won't be here much. You just go and enjoy yourselves."

More than anything I wanted them to get in the car and disappear. They fussed for another twenty minutes, then finally backed out the driveway and left.

I went into the house and locked the door. I filled up the dog-food dish to overflowing and put out a fresh bowl of water. Unfortunately Sherlock wasn't going to get outside all weekend, but he could always pee on the kitchen floor. He did that sometimes anyways. I also cleaned the kitty litter and put out enough cat food to last the weekend. Then I went up to my room and pulled out my bag of pills. I'd been putting them in a new hiding spot every day, just to be safe. This time they were taped to the bottom of my dresser. I reached down the heating vent and grabbed the bottles of cough syrup I'd stashed there, then laid everything out on my bed.

I paused and picked up my laptop. I logged on to Facebook and scanned all my friends' updates. I had 437 people listed as friends, but that was a total joke. I only ever chatted with four or five and one of them was Joe. I looked at my status box for a moment, then typed in: "Today's a good day to down a bowlful of Skittles with a Cherry Coke chaser." I hit send and shut my laptop. Then I started popping pills and chasing them down with mouthfuls of cough syrup. It was awful and nothing like Cherry Coke. It was thick and sweet and made me want to puke, so I slowed down. Throwing up would not be helpful.

The sun was starting to set and the sky glowed a soft pink. I got up to close my blinds and noticed I already felt dizzy. I took another pill and another swig of cough syrup. I shivered from the taste, then did another round. The house was still and quiet, too quiet. I went to the living room and turned on the TV. I had to lean against the wall to get back to my bedroom. My bed was soft and inviting and I sank low when I sat down on it. More pills, more cough syrup. I really wanted a drink of water but didn't want to risk watering anything down. Another round, another pause, and I started to feel unbelievably tired. I still had a handful of pills left and I didn't want to fall asleep before I got through them all, so I started swallowing two at a time.

Slow and steady, my brain instructed. You're almost there, don't screw this up.

I was starting to feel separate from brain, like I'd finally outsmarted my body and it was falling asleep. One more set of pills, one more gulp of cough syrup. My body shivered again and my head was so heavy I couldn't hold it up. I lay down on the pillow and closed my eyes. I could feel sleep tugging at me, pulling me into a dark limitless place with no movement.

*It's so easy this way*, I thought. *Why did I wait so long?*

Then there was no more thinking, just a knowing. The baggie was empty, the last bottle of cough syrup was empty, my hand was empty. Soon my brain would be empty and separate from the rest of me. At last I floated, comfortably. I felt the relief. It felt so right. Detached. I'd finally severed that one last thread that kept me tethered to my miserable life.

Sherlock came into the room and licked my hand. I told him he was a good boy, or I meant to tell him, or I thought I told him. Did I even say anything? Did I even think that? Whatever happened, he lay down beside my bed. Good ol' Sherlock. Man's best friend. Man. Friend. Best. God. I mean dog. I mean. I.

# ALIYA

When the dishes were done, I headed to my room where I was about to spend another Friday night trying not to think about what everyone else was doing. It was a waste of time trying not to feel left out though, because come Monday morning I'd be listening to all the stupid stories about who said and did what and who made out with who at Tyson's party. I knew I shouldn't feel bad and that in ten years, or whatever, nobody would remember this party, but it was hard to reason with my misery.

I logged on to Facebook and pulled up Tyson's profile page. Maybe it was just me feeling sorry for myself or trying to keep up, but I figured I might as well know the details, even if I couldn't experience them first-hand. Tyson had updated his status four hours earlier: WARNING. ALERT. PARENTS HOME AND SUSPICIOUS. NO PARTY. DO NOT CALL. DO NOT COME BY. TELL EVERYONE YOU KNOW. ABSOLUTELY NO PARTY. I guess using Facebook to announce your party is a dumb idea.

There were thirty-eight comments in response to the cancellation. Gisele's was: "This totally sucks. Nuthin 2 do now."

Farah posted: "If it wasn't so cold we could go down to the forks."

Mariam responded to Farah's comment: "Way 2 cold 2 party outside."

Kyle had posted: "Stuck home with Sam and Ray. Idiots. LOL"

I skimmed through a few more comments, but they all basically said the same things. I secretly felt a bit pleased that I wasn't the only one missing out on a crazy Friday night. Again.

Anna hadn't posted anything, which I thought was odd, so I jumped over to her profile page. She'd posted a picture of last weekend's party. It was a selfie with Mariam and Gisele, and I felt a pang of jealousy. Or maybe not jealousy, but of feeling left out at least. She'd also written: "It's a good day to down a bowlful of Skittles with a Cherry Coke chaser."

I posted a message: "You're so complex I don't even know what you mean :-P."

I knew Anna would respond for sure and I hoped Kyle would react.

I skimmed through a few more friends' profiles, but nothing new was going on so I went to the living room to watch a movie with Mom.

"What's this called?" I asked as I settled into the couch with a bowl of popcorn.

"*Thelma and Louise*. It's a classic." Mom brought us each a can of root beer and a frosty mug. I poured mine then took a drink before the foam settled.

"Check out the hair," I laughed as the movie got going.

"And the clothes," Mom added.

I didn't even recognize Brad Pitt when he came on. He looked so young. Mom had to tell me who he was, and at first I didn't believe it was really him. It was a pretty good movie, considering it was from the nineties, and I liked the soundtrack, but I had a hard time concentrating. There was something about Anna's Facebook status that kept bugging me. Something about it didn't seem right. Like, when did Anna start eating Skittles? She was a chocoholic. And Cherry Coke? Do they even still make that stuff anymore? It felt like a code, but I couldn't figure out what for.

Finally I checked my phone, but there were no new messages. Mom glanced over to let me know she didn't approve of me being on *social media*, as she calls it, while we were supposed to be having mother–daughter time so I turned my body and pretended to put my phone away. Anna hadn't replied to my message or logged any more activity on Facebook, which seemed odd since there were another twenty smartass comments since mine. That's what happens on a Friday night when everyone is stuck at home and bored out of their skulls. I figured they finally knew how I felt every weekend.

I checked to see if Anna was online, but she wasn't showing up as linked in at all. I texted but nothing came back. That's when I decided I should call her, just to put my mind at ease.

"Can you pause this for a sec?"

Mom picked up the remote and paused the movie. She looked concerned.

"I just gotta go to the bathroom. You want anything while I'm up?"

The bowl was still half full of popcorn and our mugs topped up with root beer, so Mom shook her head.

"Make it quick. We're coming to the best part."

I tucked my phone into my shirt sleeve and headed to the bathroom. I had about five minutes before Mom would start asking questions and getting nosey, and I didn't want her to know anything was up, or not up, as the case was with the cancelled party at Tyson's house.

I dialled Anna's phone while I sat on the toilet, but it went right to voice message.

"Hey, Anna. It's me. About nine-thirty. Where are you? I tried to text but you're not responding. Call me and rescue me from my mother."

I flushed the toilet and washed my hands. I checked for pimples and brushed my hair. I waited for Anna to return my call, but my phone didn't so much as vibrate. I sat on the edge of the bathtub and checked to see if she'd read my text, but she hadn't. Maybe she lost her phone or something, I reasoned. Or maybe she's busy, like really busy, like with a boy. I ran through about ten scenarios in my head but none of them made any sense.

"Aliya!" My mother called from the living room. "You okay in there?"

I went back and watched more of the movie before I decided I should try her home phone. If I could talk to her parents I might feel better. I waited a few minutes before I got up again. Mom paused the movie. Again.

"What's up with you? You're like a Mexican jumping bean."

I have no idea what a Mexican jumping bean is, but my mom compares me to one quite frequently, like whenever I move and she wants me to be still, which is a lot. She also compares me to a squirming worm and a horse with a burr under its saddle. My mom is seriously old. And weird. But

I couldn't let her know I was worried or she'd insist we drive over and check up on Anna that very minute. She believes it's better to be safe than sorry. She also lacks a sense of personal boundaries and oversteps hers daily. I could just imagine driving up to Anna's house and ringing the doorbell, then telling her parents we just wanted to check on Anna because she wasn't texting me back or trolling Facebook. It would be absurd.

"I just want to put on my PJ pants," I said. It was a lame excuse but the only one I could think of besides the bathroom, and if I went to the bathroom one more time Mom was going to insist on giving me a dose of Pepto-Bismol.

Mom sighed and hoisted herself off the couch. She headed to the kitchen and I heard the popcorn maker whirring again.

I climbed into my PJ pants as quickly as I could and at the same time called Anna's house. The phone rang and rang but nobody picked up. I ended up leaving a lame message on the answering machine that I hoped wouldn't alarm her parents if they picked it up first. Then I dialled again and it was busy. Maybe I called back too soon, I decided, and the machine was still working. I waited a minute and called again. When the machine answered, I hung up. Then I called again. And again. I called five times until I was confident nobody was home. Then I chastised myself for overreacting. Maybe I was more like my mother than I thought. Maybe I also lacked a clear sense of boundaries. Anna was probably out somewhere with her parents. They did that sometimes — went to dinner and a movie or to a play and dessert downtown.

Then suddenly on the last call, for some reason, somebody picked up. It was a man's voice, but it didn't sound familiar. He sounded panicked, though, and I panicked in return.

"Uh. Sorry. I think I have the wrong number."

"Who were you trying to call?"

"Anna."

"You have the right number. Who's this?"

"Her friend, Aliya."

"Anna can't come to the phone right now." The man sounded rushed. "Do you have a cell number for her parents?"

"No?"

"Her brother?"

"No. Why?"

"There's been an emergency."

"Who are you?" I asked, in case it was a home invader and I needed to protect Anna from halfway across the city.

"I'm Anna's neighbour. I really can't talk right now. Can you call back another time?"

I could hear voices in the background, but none that I recognized. I heard what sounded like a siren. My heart started to race and my pulse throbbed in my temple.

"Is Anna okay?"

"I don't know. Please. Call back later."

The neighbour hung up and I started to panic for real.

# ANNA

The bright light surprised me as much as it would the next person. I mean, I'd seen it on TV and read books about people going into the light, but I don't think I ever really believed it existed. And yet there it was, right in front of me. In fact, it was a little too bright.

"Can someone turn down that light?" I asked. Or maybe I just thought I asked. It was hard to be sure about anything when all I could think about was the light being too bright.

"Cripes, it doesn't have to be this bright in here, does it? Is there no consideration for the dead?" I yelled.

*Damn*, I thought. *I didn't yell. I'm thinking. Or I was thinking. I'm sure those were my thoughts, unless someone else is in here thinking with me. But I don't remember anyone else being in here. How would they even get in here?*

"I can't be dead if I'm thinking, can I?" I said.

Or maybe death is just thinking, an eternity of nothing but thinking in this bright light, I reasoned.

This isn't what I wanted.

But then I had a vague sense of being attached again, attached to that not-too-fat, not-too-ugly, completely unremarkable body. *I screwed up again*, I thought with a sinking feeling. But what could have gone wrong? Another jogger? Another highway guy? Another homeless dude? Surely Ray and Sam didn't happen to walk through my bedroom and find me? Or maybe this is, like, heaven or something and I really am dead. I considered the possibility. Maybe there *is* another level of consciousness. I wondered if I should call out for Granny and Gramps.

All the thinking was giving me a headache so I tried to put myself back into the blackness by remembering all those pills and that red syrup. I could see red, like the backs of my eyelids when I floated on an air mattress in the pool. I felt like I was floating.

"Am I in a pool, in the sunlight somewhere?" I whispered.

But no, it couldn't be. I had no plans to go swimming. And what're the odds they have pools in heaven or on another plane of existence?

*Shit, I'm going all new-age in death*, I thought. *This can't be a good sign. Did I take the wrong pills?*

The more I clawed my way back to the darkness, to the comfort of the woolly nothingness, the more I felt my senses waking up. Next thing I knew, I could feel my head cradling my thoughts, like my brain had been sucked back into my body. The more I fought to stay detached, the more I realized I was whole.

*Shit! I can feel myself breathing. I can feel my arms and my legs. My feet feel cold. Oh crap, I'm still myself and if I know I'm myself and I can feel my body, I must be alive. Did I throw up after all? Am I going to wake up in a cherry-flavoured pool of pill-studded vomit?* I wondered. I let my mouth come back to existence and tried to determine if I had that sour aftertaste, that lingering acidity. Whatever I tasted, it wasn't good, but it wasn't vomit either. My mouth felt dry and gritty and, wait, there was something there, something hard and round. It made me feel like choking.

"What the hell is in my mouth?" I tried to say.

I wanted to lift my hand to get rid of whatever was in my mouth, but I couldn't budge it. Maybe I wasn't so alive after all. That thought brought me hope.

Next my ears joined in and let me know they were working. I could hear a strange noise, like Darth Vader. And voices. I could hear voices, but I couldn't hear past the breathing sounds to tell what they were talking about.

"Excuse me, whoever you are. Do you have to breathe so loudly?" I muttered.

It didn't seem like anyone heard me. Or maybe nobody was paying attention.

Then I heard Joe's voice. It sounded like he was crying.

*I wonder if there's been an accident?* I thought. I hope Mom and Dad are okay. I hope they didn't get in a car crash on the way to their bed and breakfast.

"Wise up, Anna. You're the accident!" The words echoed in my head. "You ruined their weekend away. Loser."

"Did I think that or is there someone else in here thinking?" I asked again. It was very confusing being dead, or nearly dead, or whatever I was.

It was definitely Joe's voice I could hear on the outside, beyond the heavy breathing sound. He was saying something about the bridge last summer. Then Mom was talking.

*So I guess that confirms she didn't get in an accident after all,* I reasoned. *But how'd she get here?*

I couldn't figure out why everyone was in my room when I was trying to die.

Mom was talking about the river.

*Oh crap*, I thought. *They're going to figure it out. I'm going to get caught red-handed with those pills. Then they'll throw me into a psych ward and probably swallow the key.*

The pills. I took the pills. I was sure I took them all. I remembered seeing the empty bag. I made sure my hand was empty before I fell asleep. So why were they talking about the pills?

The thoughts scrolled through my head. There was no break between one thought and the next. It was a jumble of sounds and voices and thoughts. It was so unbearable I wished I was dead. The thought was comforting until I remembered, again, that I'd been trying to kill myself in the first place.

Oh no, Joe was crying again.

"Get it together, bro!" I shouted inside my head. "I can't stand to hear you bawling like a baby. Don't go blaming yourself. Of course it's not your fault. How could you possibly have known? Stop with the pity party, all of you! It's not like I walked around with a megaphone announcing my plans to off myself. Give your heads a shake. It just doesn't work like that. What's wrong with you people?"

I was exhausted by the anguish in the room. If I could have gotten up, I'd have run out and thrown myself off the bridge without hesitating. I should have done it when I had the chance. I wanted everyone to stop all the stupid crying.

"God, please let me go back to the blackness," I begged.

That's when I felt it creep back up on me.

"That's better," I muttered. "Maybe this was a side trip and I get to die after all."

The next time I started thinking again, it was clearer, too clear. I was definitely alive. There was no getting around it. I could feel my fingers and my toes. Whatever had been jammed in my mouth was gone, and thankfully someone had dimmed the lights. It was noisy though. There were voices and beeps, but Darth Vader was gone. There were footsteps coming toward me. But then they passed. There was a metallic clang and a smell that reminded me of something. What was it? That smell? Like the time I fell in the river and ended up in the hospital. Yeah, it smelled like a hospital.

"Shit," I said. I was beginning to like swearing, something I never did much when I was alive.

"Wait," I told myself. "I *am* alive. I'm in a hospital. Something definitely went wrong."

I couldn't escape the truth of it. I wiggled my fingers one by one, I flexed my toes. I lifted my arms, but only slightly in case someone was in the room watching or the machines started beeping. I wasn't ready for attention. After some more testing, I determined everything on my body was working.

Eventually, I knew I'd have to open my eyes too, but I wanted to put it off as long as possible. I knew she was going to be there, no matter how long I waited. Moms have some sort of superhuman capacity for sitting in hospital chairs. Even before I found the courage to look, I tried to guess the expression on her face. Confusion, fear, anger, repulsion, pity. Pick a straw.

"Anything but the pity," I begged. "Is there a barter system? I promise to keep myself alive if I can avoid the pity."

But was my life worth bartering for?

I knew there was no way I could lie there forever with my eyes closed. I couldn't hear her or smell her, but I knew she was there the way I knew I was in a hospital. It was the only thing that made sense.

I cracked my eyelids. Everything was blurry at first. Blurry and bright and it hurt when the light flooded in. Then I saw her, sitting in a chair right beside me, three feet away. She was flipping through a magazine, stopping to look at a page for a moment, then flipping to another page. She didn't seem frantic, but she looked tired. I opened my eyelids a little wider to be sure it wasn't a trick of the light. I wasn't sure I fully understood what was happening. In my mind there was still a dim possibility I was in a parallel universe and this was another mother. Finally she glanced at me. Her eyes widened. I braced myself for what was going to be an unbearable bout of tears or sympathy. But instead she smiled.

*What the hell is she smiling about?* I wondered.

I wished I could look around the room to be sure she was looking at me. Maybe there was someone behind me she was smiling at. But then she moved close. She reached out and touched my forehead. Her touch was warm and soft and I realized I'd been feeling it in my sleep. She'd probably been caressing my head for hours each day for, well, I had no idea how many days I'd been out of it.

"Anna?" she whispered softly. She was still smiling.

I murmured "hi" but I wasn't sure if anything came out of my mouth or if my throat just made the sound.

"I missed you," she said. Her voice didn't waver. I was on the lookout for any signs of fraudulent behaviour but she appeared genuinely happy.

"You're not mad?" I tried to say, but again, I couldn't tell if I'd said the words or not.

"Of course not," she said so softly I wondered if I was sharing the room with someone else, maybe someone who was sleeping.

"It's not your fault," she added.

I was baffled. Did she think I'd accidentally drunk too much cough syrup? Did she think someone forced all those pills down my throat? Did she know about the pills?

"But the pills," I managed to croak.

"I know," she said.

I wondered if they were still inside me.

"Don't worry about anything right now. The doctor said if you woke up on your own it was a good sign."

"It wasn't an accident," I whispered. I needed to know she knew the truth.

"Shhhhh. Just rest now. We can talk later. I know it wasn't an accident. But that doesn't mean you're to blame."

*Who else could be to blame?* I wondered.

She kept her hand on my forehead and the warmth seeped through me. I was so sleepy again, I welcomed the blackness as it enclosed me.

Every time I crested reality, I woke up a little more. I became aware of more, I heard more, I stayed awake longer. I also felt more. The despair was crushing. I wasn't sure what the future was going to bring, but none of the options I came up with brought me any comfort, especially knowing I had only three lines left to cross off my list, all of them unimaginable, even to me.

"You're awake again?" Mom was there. I wondered if she ever left, if she ever even went to the bathroom.

"What day is it?" I asked, trying to orient myself to being alive again.

"Tuesday."

I looked away and wanted to cry, but there weren't any tears inside me. There hadn't been for a couple of years. *Even crying would be helpful*, I thought. At least it would be something besides emptiness.

"What's wrong with me?" I wanted to ask, but I couldn't.

I also wanted to know what went wrong, but I was afraid to ask that too so I said nothing. I left it up to Mom to fill the void.

"Joe's in the waiting room. He's hoping to come in and see you now that you're talking. Is that okay?"

I sighed. I was lying flat on my back, but I could tell my head was slightly raised. I hated to think of Joe standing there looking down at me, but I nodded anyway.

"Let me go get him," Mom said.

I tried to wriggle myself upright, but it was hard. I had a wicked headache, which was ironic considering the amount of pain medication I'd taken. Then the door sighed open and Joe eased himself into the room. He looked so fragile, I was afraid if the door banged into him he'd shatter. He edged close to me and I knew he was afraid of saying or doing the wrong thing. I had days and weeks of this very same moment ahead of me, of people being afraid to get too close in case what I had was catching.

"Hey, Joe," I muttered to break the ice. It was easier to let him off the hook than Mom.

"Hey, Anna," he said and moved a little closer.

"Don't worry, it's not contagious."

He smiled, but looked like he was about to burst into tears. I decided not to give it to him for bawling earlier, when he thought I was dead, or soon to be dead.

"Where's Mom?"

"She went to get a coffee. She's been here all weekend. Even some of your friends have been by."

"Dad too?"

"Yeah, but we're not supposed to be in here at the same time. They want you to rest as much as possible."

"Are they pissed at me?"

Joe looked confused. "No."

"Liar."

"It's true." He crumpled up his eyebrows the way he does when he's trying to fix a computer or reach a new level in one of his video games.

I wanted to say something sarcastic like "too bad," but I didn't have the heart or energy.

"Why's Mom so happy?" I asked. I figured if I could be straight with anyone, it was Joe.

"Because you're alive." I couldn't tell if it was a question or a statement. It was like my brain wasn't functioning properly and I couldn't decipher emotions.

I almost smiled, or I felt like I should at least, to let him know I appreciated his honesty.

"Dad?"

"Anna, we're all … relieved. We get another chance. *You* get another chance."

"But I don't want another chance."

A hot sensation at the back of my eyes surprised me.

"You haven't been thinking right, Anna. We've been putting a lot of stuff together and the doctor thinks you've been … suffering from depression. You need to be on medication."

"That's ironic," I said. The joke was new to him, but he didn't appreciate it at all.

Joe frowned. "Yeah, I guess."

A nurse came into the room and checked the machines around my bed. I was hooked up to a bunch of equipment through all sorts of probes and patches.

"Ah, you're awake!" she said energetically. "It's nice to see you with your eyes open. Just ring if you need anything." She pointed at a buzzer attached to my bed.

When she left it took us a minute to look at each other again.

"So what happened?" I asked.

Joe took such a long breath in, I thought he might blow up like a balloon and float away.

"I mean, after I swallowed the pills. I know that part already."

"Well, Sherlock started barking. I guess he knew you were in trouble. The doctor said there's a chance you had a seizure and it might have triggered him. I guess he barked so much the Rodman's got worried and came over. They heard the TV on and the phone ringing, but they couldn't get you to answer the door so they used the spare key. When they found you unconscious, they called 911. It was the paramedics who figured it out when they saw the empty cough syrup bottles."

So Sherlock was the hero. Somehow that didn't seem so bad. At least he wouldn't be all over the news for the next three months.

"That's all?"

"Once you got here there was a bunch of other stuff. They pumped your stomach and gave you something to reverse the effects of the pills. You were on a respirator for a while because you weren't breathing on your own."

"I guess you're wondering why I did it?"

"A bit. But mostly I'm concerned about making sure you don't do it again."

I turned away. I was afraid he was going to try and extract a promise.

"Anyhow, Dad really wants to get in here and talk to you too, so I'll come back later."

They must have all been briefed by the same shrink because Dad said the same things as Joe and Mom. He said they could never be angry, just grateful I was alive, and we were all going to work together to make sure I got the treatment I needed. I would have peed myself when he said *treatment* if I wasn't hooked up to a catheter.

"When do I get to go home?" I asked after he'd stood looking at me for a few minutes without saying a word. There's nothing worse than someone standing above you, watching you lie in a hospital bed when you'd planned to be dead.

"I'm not sure, honey."

"Am I going to be okay?"

"The doctors say your body is recovering. Luckily they got to you before there was any permanent damage. Your brain seems to be functioning normally and they're confident your liver is okay."

"So, then probably pretty soon?" I asked hopefully.

# ALIYA

The news of Anna's suicide ripped across Facebook faster than a tornado across the prairies. Kyle contacted me a couple of hours after I talked to the neighbour on the phone. Somehow I'd managed to finish watching *Thelma and Louise* with my mother, which in hindsight was not a good choice of movies. Then I'd taken myself to bed in a show of sleepiness and turned off my light while my mind raced and my heart shattered, in the dark, in slow motion.

*Have you been on Facebook?* he texted.

*Yep*

It was after midnight and I hadn't taken my eyes off my phone even for a second. I was trolling Facebook, email, and text messages for information, for updates, for hope. Nothing had turned up on Joe's profile, but there were text whispers among Bachman students about an ambulance and an overdose from someone who knew someone who lived on Anna's street.

*Do you think it's true?*

*Dunno*, I lied.

I couldn't have this conversation by text with tiny words and insufficient emojis that had no connection to reality.

*Probably just someone wanting to trash her reputation. Wouldn't be the first time someone was supposedly pregnant or dead.*

*Can you get out of the house? Like now?* I felt desperate. I needed to see someone real, someone alive who I could talk to and who loved Anna as much as I did. I needed to be near someone who wasn't my mother sleeping five feet away in the next room, oblivious to the fact that my best friend was in the hospital, at best, or in the morgue, at worst.

I knew I looked like crap in my baggy PJ pants and an old sweatshirt of my mother's, but I crept through the living room and looked at myself in the hallway mirror. My eyes were beyond puffy and as red as tomato juice. I looked like I should be in bed, like I had a contagious disease, maybe pink eye or Ebola.

"Are you sick?" Kyle asked when he found me at the twenty-four-hour doughnut shop sipping on a hot chocolate. I had one waiting for him as well. He sat down and fiddled with the plastic lid, but he didn't take a drink.

"I'm not sick," I said and wiped my nose with the sleeve of my mother's sweatshirt.

The place was practically empty, just a couple of loud, blinged-out cougars eating apple fritters at a table in the corner, and some sort of construction worker in an orange vest paying for a tray of takeout coffees. The girl behind the counter looked like she wished she was in bed.

"It's true?" Kyle said in a voice so stunned and quiet it was almost a whisper.

That's when I watched reality crash into Kyle. He looked like he did the time he missed his back flip in the Christmas recital and landed on his stomach instead of on his feet. For a second he couldn't breathe.

"It's true," I squeaked. "I'm so freaked out I can't stop crying. I think I'm losing it."

"She's dead?"

I don't think he actually said the words aloud, but I must have read his lips, or his mind.

"I think she's still alive."

"She's in the hospital?"

I nodded and rested my head against the wall.

"When did you find out?"

"I read her Facebook status earlier and thought it was weird. Something about Cherry Coke and Skittles. I tried to Facebook and text and email her, but she wasn't online. Then I tried to call the house and the neighbour picked up, thinking it might be her parents. I think he called the ambulance."

"Have you talked to her parents?"

"Nobody's answering at home and her brother hasn't been on Facebook all night. I called the hospital, but all they would say was that she was admitted to the CCU. I had to pretend to be her cousin to get that much information."

"What did she do?"

"Neighbour didn't say."

"I don't get it," he said.

"I can't believe I didn't do something sooner."

"What do you mean?"

"I had a feeling something was wrong. Remember I told you guys she was acting weird? But you all thought I was being a drama queen."

"I'm sorry," he said, "I really didn't think …"

Talk about too little too late. Kyle lowered his face to the table. I saw his shoulders start to tremble so I shifted to the seat beside him and wrapped my arms around him.

"You want to get out of here?" I asked.

He nodded and sniffled. "Let's go to the hospital."

"They won't let us see her, but at least we can be nearby."

Kyle and I walked out of the doughnut shop a few minutes later. I figured if my mom woke up and noticed me missing, I'd deal with it later. Kyle texted Sam and begged him to run interference with their parents, which was an easy ask since Sam owed him about a hundred favours anyway. Then we caught a late-night bus downtown.

When we arrived at the hospital we got cups of coffee from the cafeteria and sat together in the far corner of the waiting room. We didn't say much, but being there felt like the right thing, at least at first it did.

I've met Anna's parents hundreds of times and her brother enough times to know he has a birthmark the shape of New Zealand on his back and that one of his ears is lower than the other. I've slept in their house and done cannonballs in their pool. I've eaten dinners and breakfasts and lunches in their kitchen, and sat at their table so many times I have my own placemat. But that night, I didn't recognize her mother or her father, or even Joe. I saw three people huddled on the opposite side of the waiting room. I registered fear in the set of their shoulders and the tremble of despair in their hands. But it took me by surprise when I finally heard Joe say her name and start to sob.

I nudged Kyle.

"That's her parents and her brother, Joe."

"Should we go say hi or something? At least ask how she's doing?" he asked. He sipped his coffee and stared straight ahead with a freaky intensity.

"I don't know. I'm trying to decide if they'd feel better knowing we're here or if they'd rather be left alone."

"What if they have bad news?"

"It can't be totally bad if they're still here," I pointed out. It was a grim observation, but at the moment I had my mind wrapped tightly, like the arms of a terrified child, around hope.

We watched them while we decided what to do. The only time Joe sat still was when he cried. Then he got up and paced the room. Then he left altogether. Then he came back. Then he sat down to bury his head in his hands again. Every atom of his being was in utter agony and he never once glanced our way or looked at any of the other people hunched miserably in the waiting room. Anna's father looked as stunned as I felt. Sometimes he left the room and Anna's mother would shadow Joe. She was pale. In fact, she had so little colour she looked almost transparent. Her skin seemed to glow with fear. Maybe I was reading too much into it, but I've never seen anyone look as much like a ghost as she did. I hated being there watching them, but I didn't know what else to do either.

Finally a doctor came to the edge of the waiting room, but he paused too long after he confirmed they were Anna's family, then pulled them around the corner, just beyond where Kyle and I were sitting. I strained to listen but all I heard was silence while he searched for the right words. If he'd ever had to deliver bad news before, it sure didn't seem like it. Or maybe there is no good way to deliver bad news. Either way, my blood pressure soared while he took a deep breath. I thought I was going to pass out and had to put my head between my knees.

"I think there's been a misunderstanding," Anna's mother said quickly, before the doctor could muster the courage to speak.

"There's no misunderstanding," he said quietly. "Based on the contents of her stomach, it's obvious what happened. We've done what we can, for now, but she's in critical condition."

The word *critical* came out like a whip and I shrank into my shoulders.

"All we can do is wait and see what happens. And hope she has enough fight in her to get through the next few hours."

His last line knocked me completely off balance. I felt like I'd dropped from the edge of the planet and was free-falling through space.

Kyle and I sat there for a few more minutes, and cycled up and down through our emotions so fast I think we used up a decade of energy. You know how they say your life can change in an instant? I get that now. Nothing is ever going to be the same for me, ever. Nothing is ever going to be guaranteed again: not the ground I walk on, not the fact that I will wake up in the morning with nothing more to worry about than my next exam, and especially not the fact that my friends are happy, safe, and just a short bus ride away. The cup of coffee I brought into the waiting room was like something I'd never tasted before. I'd probably sucked back forty gallons of it in the last year alone, and yet the bitter taste on my tongue was suddenly unfamiliar. Everything felt lopsided, like in one of those funhouses you see at fairs. Nothing lined up and the pieces didn't fit together. I couldn't get within a thousand miles of a reason why my very own best friend would want to hurt herself. I felt like I was being punished for something I didn't do.

After a while Kyle stood up and paced a circle in front of me. I thought he was just jittery from the coffee. But then he said, "We've got to get out of here. Let's go."

"Why?"

"I dunno. I just feel like we shouldn't be here suddenly. I've got a bad feeling."

I didn't understand, but I was too scared not to follow. I knew Kyle needed me more than Anna did at that point. When we got outside, Kyle sat down on a bench and took a huge breath of fresh air.

"I wanted to say something. Just to let them know we're thinking of her or something. But I couldn't think of what to say. Nothing seemed right. I mean, what if I said the totally wrong thing?"

I knew what he meant. It felt as if my brain had quit working. I couldn't find the right words to say, or think of the right things to do either. I felt numb with disbelief. Nothing made sense. The harder I tried to think of a good reason why Anna might have wanted to kill herself the more I realized the world was a random place, and it scared the crap out of me.

# ANNA

I begged them not to put me in the loony bin. I even managed a few tears. But they both looked at me and Mom said, "We love you too much to get this wrong."

"I've changed my mind. It's okay now," I said. "I think I was just upset about Granny and Gramps. I mean, if that stupid drunk hadn't been speeding …"

"We can't take a chance. It won't be for long. Once the medication takes effect and they think you're stable enough, they'll let you come home."

I was being transferred later that day. My new best friend, my shrink, was going to escort me because nobody thought Mom and Dad would have the guts to go through with it. If I didn't change their minds in the next five minutes, I didn't stand a chance.

"I promise. I won't try it again. I promise!" I said over and over.

"We know about the other times, sweetheart. We've been piecing things together. This wasn't an isolated incident. I hate to think where we'd be right now If just one of those five times …" She couldn't finish the sentence.

I sat stunned. I knew they didn't have to be Einstein to figure out the river incident and perhaps even the hanging. But how could they have pieced together my walk across suicide bridge and the time I scoped out the busy highway? I didn't know what to say. I wanted to defend myself, say that the bridge and highway didn't count, but I wasn't sure how much they knew and I didn't want to give anything away.

"We found your list, Anna," Dad said. He has a way of boiling things down. This time reality crashed down like a tsunami. I felt the weight land on me and threaten to flatten me to the ground. Mom finally cracked and started to cry.

"I'm sorry. I promised I wouldn't cry. I'll come see you next week and you can call us once a day," she said, then gave me a short, tight hug and left the room.

I stared at Dad. I couldn't very well throw a fit and accuse him of invading my privacy, but still, I was shocked they'd found the list and I wondered what else they'd found. Dad was pulling out all of his psychic tricks.

"We found Granny's ring too. Actually, Joe found that. And he did something with your laptop so we could see the websites you'd been to. That's what convinced us to talk to your friends, and I'm glad we did. It helped us put everything together."

I slumped into a plastic chair and buried my head in my hands.

"This is only going to make things worse. I know it. At least I had some sort of routine before. I won't be able to handle it in there with a bunch of psychos."

"They know what they're doing," Dad said firmly.

From the tone of his voice, I knew he was about to leave too.

"I love you, honey. I really do. Maybe I should have said that more …"

"It's not about being loved or not being loved," I said sullenly. It was the first time I'd let myself consider what it *was* about.

He didn't answer, but he kissed me on the cheek and then lingered a moment with his chin on the top of my head. I heard his breath catch in his throat before he turned to leave. He didn't dare look back as he went through the door.

*Maybe this is rock bottom*, I thought.

The loony bin was like a hospital and a jail rolled into one. There was no privacy and I didn't have control over anything. I got told when to wake up, when to wash, when to exercise, when to eat, when to take my medication, when to sleep. When I wasn't in group therapy or talking to the shrink, I was basically eating or sleeping or trying to avoid the other crazy people who actually belonged there. The place made me feel like I was nuts, and if I wasn't depressed before I arrived, I was a prime candidate after one day. But there was no way to hide or make excuses and there was definitely no way to kill yourself. We were supervised while we ate so we couldn't construct weapons from our cutlery. There were no knives and the dishes were made of some heavy-duty unbreakable plastic. They didn't let us wear jewellery, scarves, or belts and we couldn't wear clothing with any sort of strings or ties. I couldn't even wear a bra or underpants. And they definitely didn't let us have shoelaces, so everyone sort of shuffled and clomped around in sloppy running shoes. The noise was enough to drive me mad. I had to be supervised even when I went to the washroom, I don't know what they were afraid of me doing. There wasn't enough alcohol in my acne wipes to kill a fly and I doubt I could do much damage with a toothbrush, which was about all I was allowed to have.

When Mom and Dad came to visit the first time, I freaked out. I told them the antidepressants weren't working.

"They make me feel more desperate," I cried. "I've never felt this awful, ever.

"We'll tell the doctor, but you have to have a bit of patience. It'll take time before they build up in your system," Dad said. He sounded like a robot when he spoke. There was nothing of my actual father in the room with me other than his body. He must have had to check his emotions at the door with any sharp objects.

Mom could barely talk. When Dad stopped talking, she handed me a couple of letters she'd been holding. They felt warm and damp from her hands. She looked like a frightened rabbit. I think she was relieved when our visit was over.

The last thing I yelled at them as they left was, "It's like jail in here. You have no idea."

Then the nurse, or guard, or whoever she was, took them to see my shrink. They probably needed serious counselling after seeing me there.

The letters were from Gisele and Mariam. They were careful and short and mostly said how much they loved me and missed me, and that they would be there for me when I got home. They said I didn't have to do it alone. I appreciated that they bothered to write, but it didn't cheer me up to read them. It especially didn't cheer me up to think about having to go back to school. I knew I'd never be able to look Kyle in the face again.

I used one of my calls that week to talk to Joe. I only had ten minutes so I had to get to the point.

"I can't believe you ratted me out," I said.

"What do you mean?"

"You snooped through my room. And my computer!"

"Anna, get serious. It's not like you ate the last cookie or broke your curfew." His tone was biting and it threw me off. He'd been so understanding at the hospital.

"You're mad at me," I said. It wasn't an accusation.

"I'm not mad. But I don't understand. I want to, but I don't. I don't know what was so terrible that you wanted to kill yourself."

"Does everyone hate me?"

"Nobody hates you. We all love you. That's the point. You're my sister. The thought of losing you is — well, it's unimaginable. If you can't understand that, then you'll just have to believe me. The same way I have to believe you felt like you had a reason to do what you did. Okay? I don't want to argue. Let's just focus on getting you back to normal."

"Whatever normal is."

"It'll happen. They said in a few weeks you'll be more like your old self."

"I don't want to be my old self."

"Okay, your younger self then."

"I don't want to be any version of me."

The next week I called Joe again. Somehow it was easier talking to him than my parents. He didn't analyze every word I said, he didn't keep his tone of voice under control. I got a better sense of what he was thinking and feeling.

"Man, the people in here have some serious problems," I said.

"Like what?"

"This one girl used to get locked in a kitchen cupboard when she was a kid, while her parents went drinking. She's so messed up she literally eats the flesh off her fingers."

"That's awful."

"And this other guy is basically a paranoid schizoid. If anyone gets near him he accuses them of trying to implant probes in him. He keeps screaming that we're all part of the conspiracy and to keep away from his ears."

"Weird."

"I swear, everyone's certifiable. I don't belong at all."

"No you don't," he said.

I hadn't seen that one coming.

Every day in the loony bin was the same. They, the counsellors, forced us to talk about our feelings and we, the patients, did everything we could to avoid talking, or at least we avoided saying too much. It was like an unspoken contest to see who could say the least and get away with it. I thought I had the system all figured out, but it turned out they were just letting me settle in. Sometime during the second week they zeroed in on me. They kept asking for my opinion about things the others were saying, kept wanting me to talk about my feelings. They picked and prodded until I thought I was going to seriously lose it on them. When I couldn't stand it a second longer, when I couldn't swallow another pointed question about my stupid feelings, I screamed, "If I had feelings I wouldn't be in this freaking place!"

Nobody flinched. Either they were too caught up in their own foggy dazes or they were used to more drama than just a bit of harmless screaming.

The counsellor didn't miss a beat. He said in a deadpan voice, "So you are saying you don't feel things."

I slumped in my stinky vinyl chair. "I guess."

"That sounds like progress," the counsellor said and then turned to the cupboard girl and asked her how she felt about what I'd said.

"Fine," the cupboard girl whispered.

The following week Mom and Dad brought me a plastic container. Inside was a piece of homemade chocolate cake.

"Joe came over for his birthday last night and we saved you a piece. I know it's your favourite."

She handed it to me with a plastic fork and they watched while I devoured it.

"It's good," I said. "Thanks. The food here is worse than at the hospital."

"I guess we should have sprung for the deluxe package," Dad said and tried a tentative smile.

I nodded, then smiled back at him. "That's okay. We get popcorn every night for a snack."

Every week after that they brought me a little something, a small treat like a bag of salt-and-vinegar chips or a chocolate bar. One time they brought me running shoes with Velcro fasteners like I had in kindergarten. They were the ugliest shoes I've ever seen, but at least I didn't have to worry about kicking them off by accident if I lifted my foot off the ground.

"I know they're awful," Mom apologized. "But I thought they'd be better than what you have now."

I pulled them on and threw my old runners in the garbage can.

"They're good, thanks."

There were also more cards from Gisele and Mariam and a couple of times there were letters from Aliya. Aliya was more upbeat. I knew she was trying to cover up how she really felt, but still I laughed when she accused me of going too far to get out of our math exam. It was probably an inappropriate comment and I was sure it wouldn't have been approved by my counsellor, but it was better than everyone pretending I had the plague.

One day when we were outside for our mandatory march, which is how I thought of exercise time, I noticed it was spring. There were tulips in the flower beds and an apple tree in bloom. The petals had fallen on the ground and made a carpet of white. I sat down and picked up a petal. It was cool and soft and I rubbed it between my finger and thumb, then smelled the perfume.

"Pretty day," one of the nurses said when she came near.

"I like spring," I said.

She raised her eyebrows at me, but kept walking.

"What was that about?" I muttered. Then it came to me, slowly, like a flower yawning open in the sunshine. I was enjoying sitting on the grass among the flower petals. I was actually enjoying myself.

When Mom and Dad came the following week, I had letters for them to take back to Gisele, Mariam, and Aliya. They were short and trivial because I insisted on using a pen to write with, rather than the crayon I was allowed in my room, which means I had to write during supervised free time. That also means I didn't have much time to fuss over them.

"I'm sure the girls will be happy to get these," Mom said. "They call and ask about you a lot."

"Did you tell them when I get to come home?"

I wasn't brave enough to ask the question straight up.

"Not yet, but the doctors say you're doing really well."

"Yeah?"

"They said Joe can come and visit if you'd like."

"Does he want to?"

"Of course he does."

Joe was there next visiting day. He signed me out and we went for a walk outside. More and more I wanted to be out in the fresh air instead of breathing all that crappy institutionalized air. It was worse than the hospital, because instead of just smelling antiseptic, it was stale too. You'd think they could open a few windows now and then, especially since it was spring. But I guess they were afraid one of us would figure out how to dematerialize, squeeze through the metal grates covering the windows, and jump to our deaths.

"They don't let us out here enough. An hour in the morning and afternoon, and if you can find someone on staff to come out with you then you can manage another hour during supervised free time," I said to Joe when we got to the outside door and flung it open. I took in a huge breath, tried to get the smell of the place out of my nose.

"Supervised free time? Isn't that an oxymoron?" Joe asked.

I laughed, "I guess you're right. The whole place is an oxymoron if you ask me."

"So what's the rest of the time?"

"You mean, if it's not *supervised* free time?"

"Yeah."

"We have to be in the common room quite a bit. That way only a couple staff have to be on duty to watch us. We eat. That takes about fourteen minutes, three times a day. Then there's a lot of talking about our feelings in groups and one-on-one. We go to bed pretty early."

"Whatever they're doing, it's working, I guess."

"You think?"

"Definitely. I mean, I didn't notice it so much before, like the last year or so. I guess it was gradual. But seeing you now, you're so much lighter. You seem almost happy."

Another patient and visitor approached us on the path so we stopped talking until they passed.

"I think I feel better too. I'm sort of afraid to say that, you know? But I don't feel so, I don't know, desperate. I guess it snuck up on me and I got used to it being there. I felt like I was carrying so much weight around. It was hard to pretend that everything was okay every day."

"I'm glad you're feeling better," Joe said.

"It's not that I'm always feeling better. I mean, I felt like total crap this morning. I guess I was stressed about seeing you. But at least I have moments where something shifts and I get this little glimpse that things can be better."

"And you can talk about it."

"Yeah, I suppose. At least to you, I can. I couldn't talk to Mom and Dad like this."

"Then promise you'll talk to me. Like if you're upset or something."

"Or if I feel like killing myself?"

Joe didn't respond and I was hurt he didn't want to engage in our usual sarcastic jabs.

"It's okay to say it. It feels worse holding it in."

"Then don't hold it in," Joe said.

At my exit interview, the shrink asked me if I still had thoughts about harming myself. I was pretty sure he'd know if I was lying so I tried a bunch of answers in my head before I said anything out loud. I mean, I didn't want to get it wrong and get sent to jail without passing GO and collecting my two-hundred dollars.

"It's not that I really wanted to harm myself before. I mean, I'm terrified of pain and the thought of blood makes me pass out. It was more that I just didn't want to be alive than I wanted to kill myself."

"And now?"

"Now, even if I just had to flip a switch, I don't think I would. I still think about it. I might always *think* about it, but there's more to consider now."

"Like what?"

"My parents, my brother, my friends. There's stuff I want to do."

"Such as?"

"Get the hell out of here," I said and laughed.

He smiled. It was faint, but there it was, a little human smile.

"Seriously, I guess nothing is really any different. I always had people who loved me and needed me. I just didn't see it before. It was hard to see much of anything."

"That was the depression. You know that now, right?"

"I do, now. Yes. But it wasn't easy to see."

"That's why it's important you stay on your medication, even when you're feeling good. Especially then."

"Yeah, I get it."

"So I'll see you next week?"

"Do I have a choice?"

"Not if you want to walk out of here today."

"Then I'll see you next week. I don't think I can stomach another Monday meatloaf."

"Hang on to that thought."

# ANNA'S MOM

When my parents were killed, my email overflowed with sympathy notes. The phone rang so often we had to turn off the ringer and let the answering machine pick up. But when Anna tried to commit suicide, there was silence. Eventually her friends called for updates, but we didn't hear a peep from our family friends, and my long-time girlfriends avoided me like I was a terrorist. To tell the truth, I didn't mind the exile. It gave me time to try and order the thoughts swirling in my mind. I might have imposed the same sentence on myself anyway. Who can face listening to stories about your friends' kids when your own kid is in a mental health facility after trying to commit suicide?

While Anna was in the treatment centre I was a wreck. Had she been home with us, I could have peeked in on her and reassured myself she was still alive. But when I couldn't see her or touch her or even talk to her each day, there was a hole in my chest that nothing could soothe. I lived in constant fear that they wouldn't watch her closely enough and she'd find a way to kill herself after all. Whenever the phone rang, my blood froze. Each day when I woke up the feeling was the same: I had to catch my breath. I remembered where Anna was and my mind spit out a million questions that started with "why?" I saw the questions in my husband's eyes too, yet we didn't ask them aloud to one another. I was afraid to talk to him. I was afraid I'd detect blame in his tone and I couldn't stand the weight of any more guilt on my shoulders. I knew I was to blame without him spelling it out. It was stupid, I know, but I felt like if I could just talk to her, hug her, and tell her how much I loved her, I'd make her see reason. The psychiatrist told us many times that she didn't try to kill herself because of something we did or didn't do. He explained to us how depression is a disease and needs to be treated like any other illness — with medication and therapy. Still, I couldn't shake the feeling that I could make it all better if I tried hard enough.

During the time Anna was in treatment, a single letter came. It was from Mrs. Mahoody, an old neighbour from my childhood. I was sitting in bed, propped up against the headboard and a mound of pillows, when my husband came into the room with the mail.

"You're still in bed?" he asked when he handed me the envelope.

I glanced at the clock beside the bed. It was three in the afternoon.

"I've been up. Had lunch. Took Sherlock for a walk and all of that. I just felt chilled and came to warm up." It was sort of the truth. I'd had a coffee and let Sherlock in the backyard.

He sat down on the side of the bed and picked up my hand.

"Please don't do this," he said. "You've missed two weeks of work and you've barely stepped outside since we got home from the hospital. I can't do this alone. I need you."

I couldn't watch his eyes fill up with tears. I didn't have the strength to prop anyone up, not even myself. Instead I looked down at the shape of the comforter stretched over my knees.

"I'm sorry. I just can't face anyone right now," I whispered, surprised to hear that two weeks had already gone by. I'd forgotten to pay attention to time.

"I know you want to find someone to blame. So do I. I want to blame you. I want to blame myself. I want to blame Joe. I look at my boss and I want to blame him. But we both know it's not that simple."

My body tensed up when he said the word *blame*. My throat closed so tight I couldn't speak. So I picked up the letter from where I'd dropped it on the bed and read the return address. I fluttered the envelope in the air and my husband nodded.

"How on earth could Mrs. Mahoody have heard?"

"I guess it's not such a big city after all," he said.

My parents lived beside Mrs. Mahoody for fifty-one years, right up until they died. She watched me grow up and my kids grow up. The last time I saw her I was cleaning out my parents' house and I still called her Aunt Maggie. She brought me over a loaf of banana bread that day. She always made it special for me, the way I liked it — with chopped walnuts. When I said I couldn't believe she remembered, she laughed and said, "That's the way I like it too."

Aunt Maggie was like a second mother to me. When my mother took her extended leaves, Aunt Maggie filled the gaps. I went to her house after school until Dad got home from work and called me to come home. Then I would run across the two yards in the dark and slam into the safety of our house. When he worked late, she brought me home to give me a bath and put me in my pajamas. She'd put his dinner on a tinfoil covered plate in the oven then sit with me until he got home and kissed me goodnight. Sometimes she took me for doctor's appointments or new shoes, and I still remember her taking me to get my first real haircut at a beauty salon.

When we were together, we never talked about my mother. I was about five when Mom disappeared the first time. I asked every day where she was and when she was coming home, but Aunt Maggie always said something vague before she changed the subject. As I got older, I didn't bother to ask anymore. I knew I wasn't going to get a straight answer and I think I was afraid to find out. My father would sometimes make reference to her being in a hospital, but he'd never be able to explain what illness she had or what operation she needed, so I never believed him. When she returned home after a few weeks, she wouldn't have any visible scars or look any different. She'd hug me tight and spend long hours watching me play with my toys. She'd tell me how much she missed me. Then we'd go back to our regular routine as if nothing had happened. I'd be suspicious for a few days, maybe a week, then I guess I'd forget she'd ever been away. But I grew up not trusting what anyone told me, especially where my mother was concerned.

When my parents died, Aunt Maggie told me how much my mother loved me, how I was everything to her. I certainly didn't believe such nonsense. How could a mother, a loving mother, leave her child for weeks, even months, at a time?

When I was old enough, I suspected she was having an affair that Dad helped her cover up. I imagined she had another family and was living a double life. I'd seen it in a movie once, where the father juggled two families for years before getting caught. It made sense to me that a woman could do the same.

I was still staring at the envelope when my husband broke my concentration.

"Are you going to open it?" he asked.

I looked up, surprised he was sitting there watching me.

"I guess." I sighed.

I tore open the envelope and pulled out a piece of lined notepaper covered in Aunt Maggie's handwriting: long thin lines of cursive that was both familiar and surprising. I hadn't received a letter in years.

I'm sure the look on my face prompted my husband to look over my shoulder and read along. There had to have been horror in my eyes, if not shock.

*Dear Leslie-Marie:*

*I'm writing to tell you I'm sorry to hear about Anna being in the hospital. One of my Bingo friends is the grandmother of one of Anna's school friends and the news got to me in that roundabout way.*

*I can't imagine what you must be going through right now and I don't want to add more of a burden on you, but I feel there is something I need to come clean about. I hope it will help you understand your past better and maybe it will also shed light on your current situation.*

*I need you to understand that I never meant to lie to you. You know I love you like a daughter and would never intend to hurt you. But your mother*

asked me, she made me swear I would never tell
you what I am about to say. I don't mean to dis-
respect her wishes, but it seems now that not telling
you would be the more serious sin.

I am sure you remember the time we spent
together over the years. I still cherish that time
we had, but I regret the circumstances. When you
were just a wee thing, you always wanted to know
where your mommy was and I wish now I'd told
you. I don't know if your parents ever told you or
if they intended to and missed the chance, but
your mother suffered from depression, especially
when you were young. She was ashamed to admit
it, but she had a terrible time of it and your father
too. He was never sure when a bout would strike
her or how she would cope. Sometimes there was
no choice but to send her away for treatment.

Your mother never spoke about her time away.
I knew it couldn't have been easy for her to be
away from you or your father, not to mention the
torture she must have endured. All I know is she
was always so happy to come home to you. You
meant the world to her. She loved you more than
any mother ever loved a child.

I'm not a doctor and I am not a psychiatrist. I
can barely even understand the instructions on my
own prescription bottles these days, but I can't help
wondering if there is a connection between your
mother's depression and Anna's condition. I know
they are alike in so many other ways. As I said
before, I don't want to upset you further in any

*way and I love you like my own child, but I didn't*
*want to be the person holding on to an important*
*piece of the puzzle.*

*If you want to know more I'd be willing to tell*
*you what I can. Please call or drop by when you*
*have a chance. If it's any comfort, your mother*
*suffered less as the years went by. Her art always*
*seemed to help.*

*Love,*
*Aunt Maggie*

I knew my husband had finished reading when he sucked in his breath. By then I was on my second read-through. I must have read it ten times and each time left me feeling more confused and angry. I couldn't believe it took Anna's crisis to for me to learn the truth about my mother. Just when I thought I might be able to catch my breath, I'd get dragged under by emotions again. Suddenly I wasn't just dealing with my daughter's attempted suicide, but with my mother's history of depression and a family secret I'd never been meant to know.

"Do you think she would have seen what was happening if she'd still been around?" I asked.

My husband didn't answer, but he squeezed my hand. I knew it didn't matter either way. The truth wouldn't change a thing.

I never questioned the letter. As soon as I read it the first time, I knew it was the truth. It made sense. But the news was unexpected and because I was feeling vulnerable in the first place, I wasn't sure where to slot the information. It left me with another gaping hole and another endless set of questions I would never have answers for.

# ANNA

Let me see. There was a lot of stuff I didn't expect when I got home. There was stuff I didn't expect to find hard and stuff I didn't expect to make me happy. Then there were just plain jaw-dropping surprises. I guess the good news is that it wasn't all hard and when something difficult did happen the happy stuff usually followed.

Of course, some of it downright sucked, like walking back into school while every single person turned to stare at me. But then I didn't expect it when Kyle saw me from down the hall and walked right toward me. He didn't even flinch. It was like he didn't notice the hall had fallen, like, deathly silent.

"Hey, Kyle," I said as he approached. My words echoed off the lockers then dropped to the tile floor like bullet casings.

"Hey, Anna. You're back!" His voice sounded ridiculously happy, or maybe I was just imagining it.

"In the flesh."

"It's better that way," he said.

I laughed out loud. I was grateful there was at least one person who had the guts to face it head on.

"Are you going back to classes?"

"Well, I missed almost three months so I probably don't have a chance of passing, but yes, I'm here to try."

"Cool," he said. "I can help you with math if you want."

I'd already decided that if I was going to totally bomb one course, I'd sacrifice math. But with his offer on the table I quickly reconsidered.

A sudden hot feeling in my cheeks made me feel awkward — not embarrassed, but shy. It was like I was meeting Kyle for the first time, or seeing him for the first time. And I liked what was in front of me. Green eyes and dark curly hair, I noticed, was an irresistible combination. The heat in my cheeks doubled when I realized we were standing in the middle of the hall, staring at each other and not talking. But that's when I noticed how he was looking at me too, like I was the only person in the hall, the only one who mattered anyway. He followed me to my locker, even though I didn't say anything more to him. He didn't say anything either, but he watched me fiddle with my lock. He opened his mouth, then closed it again when the metal door creaked opened. It was like he had something to say, but couldn't find the words.

"Thanks," I said finally, in a rush. The pressure of so many emotions pushed my gratitude into the space between us. "I was afraid nobody would want to talk to me."

"It wasn't the same without you here," he said and for a split second something shifted and I got a glimpse of what I meant to someone else. I understood that, to Kyle at least, I was more than just a shadow moving through his day. I turned and looked around the hall. Some people were walking again, moving past us and to their classes, others were talking, others were stealing glances at me and Kyle.

*I'm part of this*, I thought. *I'm just one small part, but that's still something.*

Besides catching up on school work, I had other catching up to do as well. Like, I had to catch up on all the emotions I hadn't felt in so long. This was probably the most surprising thing. The colour of the green grass filled me with so much happiness one day, I thought I might explode, yet I couldn't stop staring out the window either. Talk about sensory overload.

"Anna?" Mom asked one Saturday morning when she found me standing at the bay window in the living room.

"Yeah?" I asked, but I didn't turn around.

"Are you okay?" It was a question she asked me at least ten times a day and I tried not to let it bug me.

"Uh huh."

"What are you doing?"

"Looking at the grass."

"Is there a problem with it?"

"It's so green."

She came and stood with me at the window. She probably thought my meds were making me hallucinate, but I didn't try to explain. I didn't want to interrupt the colour flooding into my brain. I could tell the grass didn't hold her attention like it did mine. Her eyes were drawn to the neighbour's flowerbeds and the birds at the feeder in our tree. Me, I just kept staring. It was so alive. Everything had been grey for so long, it was like my brain was finally broadcasting in colour again.

"Anna?" Her voice was hesitant and put me on edge. "There's something I need to tell you. Something I just found out recently."

The muscles in the back of my neck tightened and pulled me straight.

"When I was a little girl, Granny would go away some-times. She'd be gone for weeks at a time. Nobody told me where she was. Nobody would ever talk about it. But I got a letter from Mrs. Mahoody while you were away. You remember Mrs. Mahoody? Granny and Gramps's neighbour? Well, Mrs. Mahoody said Granny suffered from depression when I was little. It might have started when she was pregnant. I don't mean to upset you, but I thought you should know."

I wasn't sure where she was going with the story, but my head start to spin and I had to sit down on the couch. She sat beside me, but not too close.

"Gramps always told me she was sick and in the hospital. People didn't talk about mental illness back then, not openly anyway and definitely not in front of children."

"Did Granny take meds?"

"Apparently, yes. But I never knew. She was too ashamed to tell me, I guess. People didn't understand depression like they do today."

"It wasn't Granny's fault," I said defensively. "I mean, what if she'd been diabetic or something? Would she have been ashamed to take insulin? It's the same as any other disease."

Mom turned to look at me and I saw about two years' worth of anxiety drain out of her body. "I wish I'd known so I could have said that very thing to her. Depression can be genetic, you know. If I'd known, I might have seen the signs with you. I wish I had. I just thought it was part of being a teenager."

"How could you have known when *I* didn't even know? It's like a parasite. It gets into your head and changes you so slowly you don't even realize what's happening. Now I see how it changed everything. It turned me into someone else, someone completely different."

Food was another thing that surprised me. Whatever I ate burst into a million flavours on my tongue and after so many months, maybe years, of everything tasting bland and dry I wanted to eat everything in sight. Ice cream was sweet and creamy, the way it was supposed to be, and hamburgers, well, the first one Dad grilled on the barbeque almost blew my mind. I ate two before Mom finished one. It wasn't just my eyes and mouth on fire. Songs I'd heard twenty or thirty times suddenly had emotions attached to them, emotions I hadn't recognized before. I felt like I'd been given back my senses. I felt more alive than I could ever remember being, even though that meant feeling intense sadness and anger too sometimes.

"Honey, are you crying?" Dad asked when he found me on my bed one day after school, bawling uncontrollably. I nodded and hiccupped, then wiped my nose with the bottom of my hoodie. My eyes were hot and swollen.

"What's the matter?"

He sat with me on the bed.

"I miss Granny and Gramps," I sniffled.

"We all do, honey. We all do."

"But I just started," I said and burst into another fit of sobbing. I was out of control. But it was true. They'd been dead over two years and I was shedding my first tears.

"I guess you have a lot of catching up to do," he said.

I struggled to breath. When I finally got enough oxygen into my lungs, I managed to squeak out a few more words.

"It's a relief in a way."

"You let it all out," he said, and for a moment I was almost happy to be crying, to be feeling something. It was like the feelings, whether good or bad, made me feel connected to the world. I wasn't floating above my body like I had been before, I was solidly inside myself, feeling every last tear as it rolled down my cheek.

The anger, though, it hit with such force I wished for the numbness again. Being sad brought a certain comfort and being happy was a no-brainer, but the anger was so consuming I didn't stand a chance. I seethed with so much hate for the drunk driver that plowed into my grandparents' car, I didn't have enough space inside me to hold it all in. I had to let it out so I started throwing things. I threw the books off my bed and smashed my hand through the door. It hurt and there was blood trickling down my wrist, but my rage didn't care. I picked up my cellphone and hurled it at the wall. I didn't even flinch when it shattered into pieces. I threw my hairbrush hard against the floor and watched it bounce into my mirror, splintering it into long thin strips.

"Anna! Calm down!" Dad yelled as he pulled my hands down to my sides and wrapped his arms around me so I could only kick the air with my legs.

I flailed and screamed and kicked with all my strength until I was exhausted. Then he lowered me onto my bed and I started sobbing again. He pressed a tissue against the cuts on my knuckles to stop the bleeding, then he sat with me. I think we were both shocked by what happened.

I don't know when Mom showed up or why she enraged me again, but when she came in with a glass of water and my pills, I flung my hand toward her and sent everything flying across the room.

"It's not time yet," I shouted, even though I'd meant for it to come out gentler.

Mom took a step backward and I saw the look of horror pass between her and Dad.

"I know what you're thinking," I shouted. "You preferred the old Anna better. At least I was quiet then. You wish I was dead!"

"No," Dad said sternly.

Mom backed completely out of the room.

Then I was crying again, and begging Dad not to send me back to the loony bin.

"We're not going to send you back," Dad reassured me. "But maybe we need to move your session with the doctor to tomorrow."

He always said doctor, never something like shrink or psychiatrist. I didn't know if he couldn't face the truth or was afraid of upsetting me.

I curled into a tight ball on my bed and faced the wall while Dad rubbed my back the way he did the time I had the flu in grade five.

"I'll be right back, okay? I'm just going to make a call," he said when I was breathing calmly again.

I nodded and took a long, deep breath. I listened to his footsteps disappear down the hall. I was so worn out from my outburst I plummeted into a jittery sleep. Images and sounds were jumbled together and I couldn't make sense of anything. The homeless dude was suddenly at my side, handing me a daisy and telling me to pull the petals. When I hesitated, the jogger emerged from the fog and pulled the first one. Instead of falling over the side of the bridge though, a breeze came and the petal floated above us. I watched it swirl higher and higher.

"Go ahead and see for yourself," the jogger said, then he sprinted off into the sunlight.

The highway man was there next. He reached out and pulled another petal. It floated past the traffic and to the safety of the far ditch. I had an overwhelming urge to run and get it, but I knew it was too dangerous. Finally, Ray and Sam showed up. They ran toward me and started picking the petals so fast I pulled the daisy to my chest and told them to stop before they wrecked it.

Then I twitched myself awake. Dad was back on the edge of my bed.

*He's probably going to sit with me until I fall asleep again*, I thought, without opening my eyes.

I fell quickly into my dream again, where daisy petals were swirling all around my feet, lifting me up into the sky. I was afraid of falling and landing on the ground because it was so far down, yet still I drifted higher.

The next time I woke up, something was licking my ear. At first I thought it was Dad, but then I realized it was Sherlock. Dad wasn't on my bed at all.

"What are you doing, Sherlock?" I asked, then rolled over. "You know you're not allowed up here. Down!"

But Sherlock didn't listen. He licked my cheek frantically and squirmed closer. When I tried to roll onto my stomach and hide my face, he got me in the ear again. Sherlock has a thing for licking ears.

"Stop, Sherlock. Stop," I said.

When I opened my mouth to protest, his tongue flicked into my mouth.

"Sherlock!" I gagged.

He barked his approval and licked some more. My whole face was covered in long, wet trails of dog slobber and the more I fought to get away, the more excited he got.

Before long I couldn't help myself, I started to laugh. And the harder I laughed, the more Sherlock licked. Soon I was pinned under all seventy pounds of Sherlock, trying to fend off his lolling pink tongue.

"Okay, okay, I get it!" I squealed. "You love me!"

He licked and squirmed and licked some more.

"I love you too!" I finally said and ran my hand over his head.

He laid his chin on my chest and stared at me. I knew it was his way of worrying about me and that if I so much as twitched, he'd start licking again.

I reached down and patted his back. He licked my cheek.

"Thanks for saving me," I whispered.

He flicked his tongue across my ear.

By the time Dad came back, we were both dozing. I heard him vaguely when he walked into the room and stopped. Sherlock thumped his tail once on my bed, then lay still. Dad turned and went back down the hall. In the distance I heard him say to Mom, "She's in good hands now."

What surprised me most, I guess, when I finally calmed down, was being blindsided by the anger. I hadn't felt anything for so long, I'd forgotten what it was like to be overcome by emotions. I guess the second thing that surprised me was the calm I felt after I let it all out. Somehow the outburst — the screaming and kicking, the throwing and the sobbing — all of it left me feeling tired, yes, but quiet too. I'd felt more in an hour than I had in the previous six months. I couldn't believe I was so void before and I shivered to remember the zombie-like shell I'd been. Sure, it was tough climbing up and down through a range of emotions in one day, or one hour, but once I started to feel confident that I'd always return to a happier, more rational place, I knew I'd never lose myself completely again, that I'd always find my real self in the end.

For the first few days at home, when I felt sad, it came with deep despair. I worried I was going to feel sad forever, the way I'd felt nothing for so long, but then it would go away and, like the sun bursting from behind storm clouds, I'd feel better suddenly. Or when I felt rage over Granny and Gramps's deaths, I thought the anger would destroy me, that it would consume me from the inside out. But it didn't, it fizzled out eventually and I was back to normal again. That was what I didn't expect to find and what surprised me the most, I think — that I could not only feel emotions again but that I could find my way back to the good ones when I needed to. And that was worth living for.

# ALIYA

Even though I got home from the hospital before my mother realized I was gone, I should have known I couldn't keep it a secret from her forever. When she found out Anna tried to kill herself, she freaked out, just like I knew she would. She told me I was not to talk to Anna ever again.

"That's going to be a bit hard," I said, "especially considering she's in all my classes."

"I don't care. I don't want you under her influence."

"Mom. Get real. I'm not under anyone's influence. I'm not going to try and kill myself just because my friend did. She was depressed — medically depressed. It's an illness. She needed help and she's getting it. I'm not going to stop being her friend just because you can't handle it."

"She was such a nice girl."

"MOM! She's still a nice girl. She's sick but she's going to get better. And I'm going to be there to help her."

"Aliya, I don't …"

I couldn't listen to any more of her paranoid, old-fashioned bullshit. I did my best to be respectful, but enough was enough.

"Mom. I'm only saying this one more time. Anna is my best friend and that is not going to change. EVER. So get over it."

Then I stomped out of the living room and slammed the door to my bedroom hard enough that the downstairs neighbour banged on the ceiling with her broom handle. I stomped back at the old hag. She should turn down her hearing aid if she can't stand other people's noise.

I was really angry. I was angry at my mother for being such an idiot, but I was angry at myself too, because I'd let Anna down. Just when she needed me most, I messed up. I didn't stop her from overdosing, even when I saw the signs. I was angry that I let the others talk me out of doing something and that I let myself off the hook because I didn't want to interfere. I was so afraid of upsetting her that I never even tried to help. I didn't know what to do with all the anger I had for myself. For the first few weeks I did nothing but cry. Then I stopped feeling sad and was just plain pissed.

When Mariam and Gisele told me they were sending Anna letters and that I should write one too, I said no.

"What do you mean, 'no'?" Mariam asked.

"I don't know what to say. What if I say something I shouldn't?"

I didn't want to tell them I was too upset to write.

"It's not like you have to write a Pulitzer Prize–winning novel. Just tell her you miss her and you hope she's feeling better," Gisele said.

"She's not stupid. If I say something lame like that she's going to see right through it."

"If you don't write at all, she's going to see through that too," Mariam said.

I knew they had a point, but I was afraid of letting anything negative slip through. She didn't need to know I was feeling guilty and mad at myself. I didn't want to dump anymore anxiety on her and part of me wondered if she was still the same Anna. I mean, I knew a guy who was in a terrible car crash once and even though the following year he came back to junior high looking exactly the same, he wasn't the same at all. He didn't remember anyone's name and his personality had done a one-eighty. He wasn't the same outgoing guy anymore and he didn't crack jokes. When I introduced myself and reminded him about the time we did the skipping routine at the spring talent show the previous year, he just looked at me blankly as if he was looking through me. It was like his memory had been erased, and it creeped me out so much I never spoke to him again. I felt bad not talking to him that year, but he just gave me the willies.

I did manage to send Anna a couple of letters in the end. After about twenty false starts I got into a rhythm. I imagined we were Facebooking and that she was sitting on her bed with her laptop. It helped to picture her there instead of in some unimaginable hospital with crazy people all around her. Still, just because we exchanged a few letters, I wasn't convinced she'd be her regular self and I was super nervous about seeing her for the first time. Part of me worried she'd be mad at me too, for not helping her. She must have felt the same way about seeing me because her mother called and invited me over the weekend she came home. Her mother said a short visit was exactly what Anna needed and asked if I could come over Saturday afternoon.

"Is there anything — well, anything I need to know before I come?" I asked.

"Just that she's missed you. I'm sure she'll want to keep it light, but you don't have to worry, she's doing great. We thought if she saw a few of her friends before she went back to school, it would make the transition easier."

I agreed to be there at two. But as soon as I hung up I started dreading the visit. I almost wished my mom wouldn't let me go, but after our fight, she'd dropped the subject completely. I guess I can be convincing when I want to be.

Anna was watching TV when I arrived. Other than the fact that she was a little pale, she looked great. She stood up and we hugged before we even said one word. Then she said, "I missed you."

"I missed you too," I said. I looked her in the eyes but it was hard. My gut reaction was to turn and run.

Ann must have sensed I was feeling uncomfortable because she quickly said, "Thanks for writing."

"No problem. It was weird though. I haven't written a letter since my grandmother finally got an email account."

"They wouldn't let us online."

"No, I guess they couldn't."

I looked out the window and wondered how long I should stay.

"You want to sit down?" Anna asked. Then she sat down on the couch with her feet tucked under her. I looked at the couch, then at the armchair. In the end I sat down on the other end of the couch. I searched for the next thing to say, but her mother saved us.

"Aliya, thanks for coming by. Can I get you something to drink?"

"Sure, I guess," I said and looked at Anna to see if she was going to ask for something.

"Is there any Coke left?"

"Of course. I'll bring a couple of glasses," her mother said and left again.

"So how are you feeling?" I asked. As soon as I said it I wished I could take it back. It was too obvious.

"I'm okay."

"You look good."

"You think?"

"You always look good."

Anna rolled her eyes, smirked, and said, "Whatever."

"Are you going back to school?"

"Yeah. Next week. I'm supposed to take it slow."

"Did you see Mariam or Gisele yet?"

"Maybe tomorrow."

"You want me to pick you up the first day?"

"Mom's bringing me. We have an appointment with the principal first."

"We can meet up for lunch."

"For sure."

We stopped talking when her mother came in the room and handed us each a glass. I took a sip and so did Anna. When her mother left, she cleared her throat like she had something important to say.

"I'm kind of scared about going back."

"It'll be fine. You'll get back in the swing of things in no time. Besides, you won't be alone."

"I guess. At least I have you."

"You have all of us. You always did." There was a bit of an edge to my tone, an edge I hadn't intended and it made me cringe. I hoped she hadn't noticed it.

"Are you mad at me?"

I sighed. Nobody told me if I was supposed to tell the truth or say the right thing. Still, it wasn't like me to lie.

"I was. I don't know. Maybe I still am. But I don't want to be." The truth choked me and I had to take a sip of Coke to clear my throat.

"I'm sorry. I didn't mean to put everyone through so much."

"It's not your fault," I said and made patterns in the condensation on the outside of my glass.

"No, but I still feel bad."

Anna lowered her head and studied the glass her hands. I knew I had to get my feelings out in the open or the moment would be lost and our friendship would never be the same.

"I'm more mad at myself."

"Why would you be mad at yourself?"

"Because I didn't do anything to help. I didn't stop you."

"How could you have?"

"I should have tried talking to you. I thought something was wrong."

For the hundredth time I thought about my conversation with Mariam, Gisele, and Kyle in the school cafeteria and for the hundredth time I couldn't believe I let them blow me off.

"It wouldn't have made a difference. I wouldn't have talked to you anyway. I didn't even realize what was going on. I thought everyone felt the way I did."

"That's why I wish you'd talked to me."

"It's not that simple," Anna said.

"But you didn't even give me a chance."

"So that's why you're angry?"

"I guess."

"Don't beat yourself up. I didn't give myself a chance either," she said.

# ANNA

Mom and Dad agreed to let me have a pool party on the last day of school and the weather, like, totally cooperated. It was one of those days where it seemed the sun couldn't get enough of shining and there wasn't even a whisper of a breeze. The party hadn't been my idea, and at first I hated the thought of being practically naked and wet in front of so many people, but Mariam and Gisele pestered me relentlessly because I was the only one with a backyard big enough. Finally I said yes just to shut them up. Then I made them promise to help set up, clean up, and not leave me standing alone without anyone to talk to.

The day of the party Mariam and Aliya came home with me on the bus. We made nacho dip and cheese and veggie trays and spread the whole picnic table with food. We strung Christmas lights along the fence for when it got dark and filled a cooler full of ice and drinks. Then we set up the most awesome playlist on my iPod.

Gisele was the first to arrive and bounced into the house with a gigantic hoot. Then she looked embarrassed and asked, "Are your parents home?"

I laughed. "No, they're both at work, then they're going out to dinner and a movie. They won't get home until after eleven."

"Sa-weet," she said and threw off her skirt and tank top. "Let's go for a swim."

"What a hottie!" I said when I saw her in the cutest-ever bikini. It was blue with black Hawaiian flowers and the bottom was like a pair of shorts.

"Yeah, right," she said and flicked her towel at me.

"Seriously," I said. "You look awesome."

"I guess that means something coming from the queen hottie biscotti herself," Aliya said.

I must have looked confused because before I could come up with something to say back, Gisele burst out with, "That's the thing I love most about Anna. She doesn't even know she's, like, a total catch."

"Whatever," I said and rolled my eyes.

"Why else do you think Kyle's had his eyes glued to you for the past three years?" Aliya asked.

"You think he likes me? Really?"

"No, I think he loves math so much he wanted to share the joy of algebra with you," Aliya said and they all burst out laughing.

"Okay, enough," I said. "Let's go for a swim." I wasn't sure I'd have the courage to go in the pool when everyone arrived and I wanted the chance to at least get wet at my own pool party.

We changed into our suits and I left a note on the front door telling people to come through to the back, then we all went and jumped in the pool. The water was the perfect temperature — cool enough to be refreshing, but not so cool you felt chilled after a few minutes. Once we were wet we each climbed on an air mattress and rafted together to float in the sun. The others lay on their stomachs, but I lay on my back and looked up at the sky. It was so blue I could have stared at it all day. Music filled the backyard and it felt like the whole city had drifted away, that it was only us in the pool, in our own private world.

"When's Sam getting here?" Aliya teased Mariam.

"Soon, I think," she said. "He and Kyle had to go home and do something for their dad first. Then they're coming over."

"Is Ray coming?" Gisele asked.

"Of course," Mariam said and splashed her. "Try and keep your cool."

I thought a major splash session was going to erupt, but everyone went back to their own thoughts. We floated in the sun until Sherlock started barking his happy bark. The back door creaked open and slammed shut. The girls lifted their heads until I said, "Relax, it's just Joe."

Joe and Jamal were already in their swim shorts. When I saw them pick up speed and run toward the deep end, I knew what they were about to do. I slipped off my air mattress and when I came up from under the water, the girls were yelling and Joe and Jamal were laughing. For a skinny guy, Joe can do sick cannonballs.

Kids started arriving and soon the backyard was packed. I think most of the grade elevens were there, and quite a few of the grade twelves. There were even a few kids from Sam and Ray's school. I was sort of relieved that Joe and Jamal had come over to keep things under control.

I felt jittery when I spotted Kyle coming through the back door and was glad I had put my T-shirt and shorts back on. I was at the picnic table digging into the nacho dip when I saw Sherlock giving him the once over.

"Don't worry," I called out, "he's a total suck. Wouldn't hurt a fly."

Kyle put his hand out for Sherlock to sniff and Sherlock took it as an invitation. He started licking Kyle's hand and up his arm. Kyle laughed. It's hard not to laugh when a great big dog licks you like that.

"Sherlock!" I scolded. "Go lie down."

"It's okay," Kyle said. "I like dogs."

When Kyle rubbed Sherlock's ears, Sherlock dropped to the ground and rolled over on his back. Kyle gave him a quick belly rub, then looked at me. I felt myself blushing.

"You've got a really nice house," he said.

I looked around and noticed that it *was* a nice house.

"Yeah, thanks. I guess I'm lucky," I said.

Joe saved me from the awkward silence that might have followed because he was suddenly at my side, introducing himself to Kyle.

"Are you two close?" Kyle asked, after Joe finished interrogating him and went to find Jamal.

"I guess so. We Facebook a lot. Tease each other. That sort of thing."

"He's not an idiot like Sam, I take it?"

I laughed. "No, he's pretty mild compared to Sam."

"You're lucky."

Even though Kyle had coached me through math for six weeks, I still felt awkward talking to him. It was fine when we were discussing algebra equations, but as soon as it came to making conversation, my mind froze and I started to worry about what he was thinking of me. I usually worried that he wouldn't like me if he got to know me and then I could never think of anything clever to say. When I felt my brain threatening to seize up on me, I excused myself. I told Kyle I had to run inside and would be right back. Kyle smiled graciously and headed over to the pool to talk to some of the guys.

I went into the kitchen and came back out with bowls of nacho chips and cheese-flavoured popcorn. I also reloaded the veggie tray. Then I went upstairs to the bathroom. I could hear the music drifting in through the open windows and the swell of conversation. There were squeals and splashes and a lot of laughter. I wandered into the spare bedroom and looked out at all the activity. Sam and Mariam were lying on an air mattress together in the deep end and Ray was trying to tip them into the water. Farah was talking to Tyson by the picnic table and Jamal was getting ready to do a trick off the diving board.

I saw Joe looking at the playlist on my iPod. I wanted to yell out the window and tell him to keep his paws off my music, but I knew he'd never be able to hear.

Several girls were sitting on the edge of the pool, kicking water at a group of boys. There were kids on the lawn chairs and kids sprawled out on towels in the grass. Sherlock was sneaking through the crowd, licking any ears he could find. I couldn't believe so many kids had come to *my* party.

I looked back at the pool. Kyle was in the shallow end, floating on a pool noodle and talking to Aliya. He looked up and saw me in the window. He smiled, then waved. Aliya looked up too.

"Come on in!" Aliya shouted.

I nodded, but I didn't move right away. I couldn't. I felt flooded with so much happiness I didn't want to miss a drop. It was like a fire hose had been suddenly turned on and was filling me to the top.

Kyle looked up again.

"Hurry up!" he yelled.

I waved and called out, "I'm coming."

That's when I remembered the guy who'd hanged himself at Halloween. I remembered thinking at the time that he'd had a good reason and suddenly I couldn't believe such a thought had actually crossed my mind. There's no good reason to miss the rest of your life, I realized. I also thought about the legless girl and the faceless boy. When they'd talked about being filled with happiness and finding purpose in their lives, I couldn't grasp it at the time. I couldn't begin to understand how they managed to feel happy when they had to live without parts of their bodies and the knowledge that they had failed so miserably in trying to kill themselves. But suddenly, with the warm summer air drifting in through the window and the sounds of a party going on outside, *my* party, I felt so attached to everyone that I glimpsed their meaning, ever so briefly. I understood that they didn't see it as failure but as a second chance, that they had been spared, had been given the gift to live on. The understanding was fleeting, but in a part of a second, a sliver of time, I felt connected to the kids outside, to my neighbourhood, to the city, to the world. I felt like I belonged to the kids outside my house, to my teachers, to my parents, to the people I didn't even know but who I saw every day, like the man who drove the bus I took to school. I tried to think if I'd ever said hello to him or offered him a smile. I couldn't picture his face and yet I'd ridden the same bus for almost three years.

I crossed the hall and looked around my bedroom. It looked happy and inviting with the sunshine flooding in through the window. I loved the new comforter Mom had bought at one of her sales. It was white with giant blue, pink, and lime-green circles. She'd bought new pillows to go with it too. My math binder was lying on my desk, but I already knew the list was gone. I checked when I first got home. Thanks to Kyle, math was the only class I managed to pass. But I knew it didn't matter, I had the summer to make up the other classes so I could still graduate with everyone next year. I looked at myself in the mirror and took off my T-shirt and shorts. I did look good in my bathing suit. It was a one-piece, not a bikini like the other girls were wearing, but still, I realized, I looked fit and tanned.

For a moment I just wanted to stretch out on my bed and listen to the commotion going on outside, but then I heard Joe calling my name. I knew he wanted to change the music and there was no way he was going to put on his crappy rap music and ruin my party.

"Coming!" I shouted as loud as I could, "Joe! *Don't you dare* touch my iPod."

I twisted the ring on my finger — Granny's ring that Joe had rescued for me and Dad took to get resized. Whenever I felt it I knew Granny and Gramps were watching me from somewhere and cheering me on, that they wanted me to live. I looked up and smiled. Then I raced down the stairs and headed straight for the pool.